She knew ___ "nice" and ___ "okay" and soul-inspiring wonderful.

And Simon Sheffield with his mind-blowing mouth definitely fell into the latter category.

With her lips no longer hermetically sealed to his, Kennon had to concentrate on catching her breath. It felt as if she had just completed a twenty-six-mile marathon inside of a time warp. Her head was spinning badly. It was a huge effort to get her mind back in gear, because right now there were rainbows and fireworks flashing through it and absolutely *nothing* that anyone with even a minimally developed brain could mistake for a thought.

Other than wanting to kiss him again.

Damn it, get hold of yourself. You're not some starry-eyed teenager—and neither is he.

But that was just the problem. She *did* feel starry-eyed. And the racing pulse, the sweaty palms, the shortness of breath, they *all* belonged to a naive, inexperienced teenager.

What had he done to her?

Dear Reader,

Thought you were done with the series, didn't you? But…well, I've said it before. I'm not good at saying goodbye, so here we are again, watching Maizie Somers, full-time Realtor, full-time mom, weave her magic and come to the rescue of yet another concerned mother who cannot understand why her smart, pretty, vibrant daughter doesn't have a ring on her finger and babies in her house. Lucky for the concerned mother—who just happens to be Maizie's former sister-in-law—there are two motherless children in the background, as well, rooting for their dad to find the perfect mom to love them.

Kennon Cassidy is an interior decorator who takes houses and turns them into homes—for other people. That is, until Maizie sells a house to Dr. Simon Sheffield, a handsome, widower doctor who is emotionally adrift ever since he lost his wife. Isolated in his world of pain, he cannot even connect with the young daughters he loves. He doesn't know how. Until Kennon shows him the way. And this time around, everyone, including Kennon, reaps the rewards.

Thank you for taking the time to read this book and, as ever, I wish you someone to love who loves you back.

Marie Ferrarella

A MATCH FOR THE DOCTOR

MARIE FERRARELLA

™ Harlequin®

SPECIAL EDITION

Recycling programs
for this product may
not exist in your area.

ISBN-13: 978-0-373-65599-1

A MATCH FOR THE DOCTOR

Copyright © 2011 by Marie Rydzynski-Ferrarella

www.Harlequin.com

Printed in U.S.A.

Ruth glared at her, then exhaled loudly in exasperation. "All right, maybe I had that coming."

"Maybe?" Maizie echoed softly, an amused eyebrow raising high over crystal-blue eyes.

Ruth threw up her hands in desperation. "All right, I *did* have that coming. That, and maybe even more." The words seemed to burn on her tongue, but she pushed on. "I'm sorry, but I always thought you stole Terrence away from what would have been a very good match for him. Sandra Herrington was wealthy and her family went all the way back to the *Mayflower*."

Maizie was well aware of her former rival's pedigree—and the fact that her late husband always swore she'd saved him from an eternity of unspeakable boredom. But, for the sake of peace, she said enigmatically, "Yes, I know."

Ruth frowned. "I was wrong, okay?"

Maizie had never thought of herself as a genius, but she was also far from stupid or gullible. "You're only saying that because you want my help."

About to deny Maizie's assumption, Ruth finally shrugged in a helpless manner. "Well, it's a start, isn't it?" she asked. "I'm sorry, I made a mistake coming here. It's just that I heard that you and your friends were running some kind of matchmaking service on the side—"

Maizie shook her head. It absolutely amazed her how rumors were born out of twisted half-truths.

"It's not a 'service,'" she corrected. "Since Theresa, Cecilia and I have our own businesses in very public-oriented fields," she said, referring to her two very best friends, women she'd known and been close to since the third grade, "we just decided to keep our eyes open for possible suitable matches for our daughters." She smiled, exceedingly pleased. Plumbing the depths of their client lists for eligible men had been her idea initially and it had succeeded far better than she'd ever dreamed. All three of their daughters, plus Theresa's son, Kullen, had been gently nudged into relationships that now had every indication of lasting forever. "As it turned out, things went well."

Ruth sank down in the chair again, her dark eyes riveted to her sister-in-law's face. "I need them to 'go well' for Kennon. The way things are going, after that horrible man she wasted all those years on decided he loved someone else and just dumped her, Kennon has done nothing but work. She hasn't gone out on a date even once in almost a year. I don't want her to wind up alone," Ruth concluded with sincerity.

"No dates at all?" Maizie repeated. God, did that ever sound familiar. "She told you this?"

"A mother knows," Ruth informed her. She further relayed how she "knew" because she'd gone out of her way to draw Kennon's assistant, Nathan, into her camp. She'd won the young man over with her coconut cream pies, exchanging them for information.

The wheels in Maizie's head were already turning as inherent instincts, centuries old, rose now to the fore. "Does Kennon still own that interior decorating shop?"

"She all but lives there." Seeing the look in Maizie's eyes, Ruth slid to the edge of her chair, hope taking hold. "Why? What are you thinking?"

"As it happens, I just sold a beautiful, empty house to a newly transplanted widower. He needs a decorator badly." Maizie hit several keys on her computer, pulling

Selected Books by Marie Ferrarella

Special Edition

°*Mother in Training* #1785
Romancing the Teacher #1826
§§*Remodeling the Bachelor* #1845
§§*Taming the Playboy* #1856
§§*Capturing the Millionaire* #1863
°°*Falling for the M.D.* #1873
~*Diamond in the Rough* #1910
~*The Bride with No Name* #1917
~*Mistletoe and Miracles* #1941
††*Plain Jane and the Playboy* #1946
~*Travis's Appeal* #1958
§*Loving the Right Brother* #1977
The 39-Year-Old Virgin #1983
~*A Lawman for Christmas* #2006
¤¤*Prescription for Romance* #2017
¶*Doctoring the Single Dad* #2031
¶*Fixed Up with Mr. Right?* #2041
¶*Finding Happily-Ever-After* #2060
¶*Unwrapping the Playboy* #2084
°*Fortune's Just Desserts* #2107
¶*A Match for the Doctor* #2117

°Talk of the Neighborhood
*Cavanaugh Justice
†The Doctors Pulaski
§§The Sons of Lily Moreau
°°The Wilder Family
~Kate's Boys
††The Fortunes of Texas:
    Return to Red Rock
¤¤The Baby Chase
¶Matchmaking Mamas
°The Fortunes of Texas: Lost…and Found

Romantic Suspense

The Heart of a Ruler #1412
**The Woman Who Wasn't There* #1415
*Cavanaugh Watch #1431
†*Her Lawman on Call* #1451
†*Diagnosis: Danger* #1460
My Spy #1472
†*Her Sworn Protector* #1491
*Cavanaugh Heat #1499
†*A Doctor's Secret* #1503
†*Secret Agent Affair* #1511
**Protecting His Witness* #1515
Colton's Secret Service #1528
The Heiress's 2-Week Affair #1556
*Cavanaugh Pride #1571
**Becoming a Cavanaugh* #1575
The Agent's Secret Baby #1580
**The Cavanaugh Code* #1587
**In Bed with the Badge* #1596
**Cavanaugh Judgment* #1612
Colton by Marriage #1616
**Cavanaugh Reunion* #1623
***In His Protective Custody* #1644

American Romance

Pocketful of Rainbows #145
°°*The Sheriff's Christmas Surprise* #1329
°°*Ramona and the Renegade* #1338
°°*The Doctor's Forever Family* #1346

MARIE FERRARELLA

This *USA TODAY* bestselling and RITA® Award-winning author has written more than two hundred books for Harlequin and Silhouette Books, some under the name Marie Nicole. Her romances are beloved by fans worldwide. Visit her website at www.marieferrarella.com.

To
Stella Bagwell,
for her sweetness,
her friendship,
and
her continuing patience with me

Prologue

Maizie Sommers leaned back in her chair, silently observing the somber-faced, stylishly dressed woman who had marched into her real-estate office, quite obviously on a mission.

Few things surprised Maizie these days, but this had. She hadn't said a word since the woman entered and started talking. That was almost ten minutes ago, and she was still talking.

Ruth Cassidy, her senior by some three years, was not in the market either to buy or sell a house. She was in the market for a man. Specifically, for a husband. More specifically, a husband for her beautiful and exceedingly selective twenty-eight-year-old daughter, Kennon.

Although Maizie hadn't seen the young woman very often in the last fifteen years, she had always been very fond of Kennon, who was her late husband's niece.

As for being fond of Ruth, well, not so much. But that had been both Ruth's choice as well as her fault.

Ruth had made it very clear, right from the beginning, that she didn't approve of Maizie or think that she was good enough for her older brother, Terrence.

Ruth never called him Terry, the way she did, Maizie remembered.

As Ruth gave every sign of droning on, Maizie suddenly placed her hands on the padded armrests, pushed down and rose from the Italian leather chair she'd had specially made for her. It had been her first frivolous purchase. If she needed to put in long hours at her desk, she intended to be comfortable doing it.

Without a word, Maizie walked over to the front window. She looked out onto the main thoroughfare that passed by the office, searching for something.

Ruth twisted around to get a better view of her former sister-in-law. "What are you doing?" she asked sharply.

Maizie didn't turn around but continued gazing out the window as she quietly replied, "Looking to see which of the horsemen is first."

"What horsemen? What are you *talking* about?" On her feet now, Ruth stared out through the window herself at the usual midmorning traffic.

"The Four Horsemen of the Apocalypse," Maizie replied. She turned away from the window to face Ruth. Her sister-in-law still had her looks. And still retained that superior attitude. "The way I see it, since you're here, talking to me, asking for a favor, either hell is freezing over or the end of the world is coming, and I can't see hell from my window."

up the information she needed. "He just moved here from the San Francisco area. The man has two small daughters." Maizie watched her former sister-in-law's face to see her reaction.

It was apparent that Ruth saw potential here. "A jump start on becoming a grandmother. I can live with that." She leaned in closer. "What does he do for a living?"

Maizie smiled. "He's a cardiovascular surgeon."

"A doctor?" Ruth cried. She began to glow with enthusiasm. "Maizie, I think I love you. All is forgiven."

"Nice to know," Maizie said dryly.

Sarcasm had always been wasted on her late husband's sister. Now was no exception.

Some things never changed, Maizie thought as she looked up Dr. Simon Sheffield's cell phone number.

Chapter One

"Good God, woman, have you been here all night?"

The partially perturbed, partially breathless question shot out of Nathan LeBeau's mouth ten seconds after he'd flipped on the light switch in the back office and subsequently jumped when he saw something moving on the white leather sofa. Nathan's thin, aristocratic hand was dramatically splayed over his shallow chest in the approximate region of his heart, presumably to keep it from leaping out of said chest.

"How am I supposed to impress you with my hard work when you keep insisting on being an overachiever and staying here until all hours of the night?" He went to the office's lone window and drew back the light blue vertical blinds. "You're lucky you're not dialing 9-1-1 right now."

"Why would I be dialing 9-1-1?" Kennon Cassidy murmured, trying to clear the cobwebs out of her brain, the sugary taste out of her mouth and the protesting kinks out of her shoulders. She had little success in any of the endeavors.

"Because you scared me half to death," Nathan informed her with a toss of his deep chestnut mane. Blessed with incredibly thick hair, Nathan deliberately wore it long, in the fashion of a driven music conductor.

Nathan's words were addressed to Kennon Cassidy, technically his employer, more aptly described as his friend and, initially, his mentor.

Kennon sat up on the sofa and looked up at her tall and more than occasionally judgmental assistant. "What time is it?"

Nathan scrutinized her attire. "I'd say way past the time when your carriage turned into a pumpkin, standing in the field next to your musically gifted pet mice."

Kennon waved a dismissive hand in his direction. "You've been watching way too many classic cartoons, Nathan."

"Not by choice," he said defensively. "Judith insists that's all I can let Rebecca and Stuart watch when I babysit the little darlings. Can't wait until those two hit puberty and stage a revolt on my straitlaced sister."

Nathan put his hand on his hip expectantly as he regarded the slender, slightly rumpled blonde who had taken a chance on him when he had bluffed his way into the office four years ago. "You really need to move on, you know."

Her eyes met his. There was no way she was having this discussion. "No, I really need to get rid of this sugary taste," she told him. "Apparently I fell asleep with a cough drop in my mouth."

Rising, Kennon caught her reflection in the window.

She shuddered. God, she looked like death warmed over. *Barely* warmed over.

The next second, she stifled a yawn while trying to remember when she'd fallen asleep. "I just lay down on the sofa for a minute to close my eyes."

"Apparently you succeeded beyond your wildest dreams."

"What time is it?" she asked Nathan, this time in earnest. "Really," she underlined.

"It's tomorrow," Nathan answered. When she looked at him quizzically he backtracked for her benefit. "Tuesday. Eight-thirty a.m. May fourth. The year of our Lord, two thousand—"

Kennon threw her hand up in the air to stop him. Nathan had the ability to go on and *on* if she let him.

"I know what year it is, Nathan," she informed him. "I'm not exactly Rip Van Winkle, you know."

"I hear he started out by taking long naps," Nathan told her dryly. He glanced at the open sketchbook she was currently using. "Were you working on the Prestons' house?"

That had been her initial intent. But what she'd really been working on was her self-esteem. Although she loved Nathan like the brother she'd never had, she was *not* about to dwell on that point for him. It was bad enough that her assistant knew about her breakup with Pete, or rather, Pete's breakup with her, since Pete had been the one to end the relationship and walk out. Granted, she hadn't been head-over-heels, can't-seem-to-catch-my-breath in love with the man, but it bothered her to no end that she hadn't seen the breakup coming.

One morning, after living with her for two years, Pete announced that he'd fallen "out of love" with her. And in love with some big-eyed, bigger-breasted, conscienceless little blonde whom he had the absolute gall to marry six short weeks after blowing a hole in her world.

Since she'd been so drastically wrong about the man she'd assumed she was going to marry, Kennon began to doubt her ability to make *any* kind of a decent judgment call.

She was finally putting her life back in order when she heard that Pete and his wife were expecting. It had hit her harder than she'd thought. She had a real weak spot when it came to children.

"Yes, I was," she replied, thinking it best just to go along with the excuse Nathan had just handed her. "I was working on the Preston home."

He pushed the sketchbook aside, clearly indicating that he saw nothing worthy of her expertise. "Okay, let's see it."

The truth was, she had nothing to show for her efforts. She'd come up with better ideas her first year in college. "See what?" she asked vaguely.

"See what you've come up with," Nathan said patiently.

"I think you've got this turned around, Nathan. I sign your checks, you don't sign mine."

"You also didn't come up with anything, did you?" he asked.

She shrugged, looking away. "Nothing worth my time."

"And that would apply to a broad spectrum of things," he replied, circling her so that she could get the benefit of his pointed look.

She knew Nathan meant well, but he needed to back

off for now. "Nathan, I've already got one mother. I don't need two."

"Good, because you don't have two," he told her briskly. "I'm just a friend who doesn't want to see you wasting your time, missing a guy you shouldn't have given the time of day to in the first place."

She'd given Pete more than the time of day. She'd given him over two years of her life, she thought angrily.

"I don't want to talk about him," she said firmly.

Nathan nodded approvingly. "Good, because neither do I. Now splash some water in your face, put on some makeup and change your clothes," he instructed. As he spoke, he opened a cabinet that ordinarily contained hanging files but now held a navy-blue pinstripe skirt and a white short-sleeved oval-neck top.

Whipping them out on their hangers, Nathan held the prizes aloft before her, even as he put one hand to the small of her back. He propelled her toward the bathroom. "We want you looking your best."

Kennon stopped dead. "We? Exactly what 'we' are you referring to?"

"Why, you and me 'we,' of course," he said, trying to sound innocently cheerful. "You always this suspicious this early in the morning?"

She took the clothes from him. "I am when you suddenly start acting like a social directing steamroller."

"Fine." Nathan held up his hands in surrender, backing away from her. "Look like an unmade bed and scare away our customers. See if I care. I can always go back to sleeping on my sister's couch, having those little monsters jump up and down on me in those awful pajamas with the rubber bumps on the bottoms of their hard little feet."

She capitulated. If she didn't give up, the drama would only get worse. "I'll splash water in my face, put on some makeup and change my clothes," she sighed.

"That's my girl," Nathan declared with a grin.

She gave him an unsettled, puzzled look as she slipped into the pearl-blue-tiled bathroom and closed the door.

"By the way," he addressed the door in a matter-of-fact voice that wouldn't have fooled a two-year-old, "You're meeting a client in Newport Beach in an hour."

An hour? Nothing she hated more than being rushed.

And then she remembered.

"I didn't *make* an appointment with a client for this morning," she informed Nathan through the door.

"I know. I did."

It wasn't that Nathan couldn't make appointments. But whenever he did, he always told her. Bragged was more like it. He took extreme pleasure in being able to say he carried his own weight and drew in clients.

"When?" she asked. "I was here all day yesterday— and last night. I didn't hear you making an appointment and no one new called the office."

"It's a referral," he told her.

Dressed, Kennon opened the door so she could look at Nathan. She began to apply her makeup.

"Oh? From who?" Kennon flicked a hint of blush across her pale cheeks. She needed to get some sun time.

"What does it matter?" Nathan said with a quick rise

and fall of his shoulder. "One happy, satisfied customer is like another. The main thing is the referral."

She put down her lipstick tube. Something was rotten in the state of Denmark. "From who?" she asked again. Nathan was being incredibly mysterious—even for Nathan.

"Initially, your aunt Maizie," he said evasively.

"Initially," Kennon repeated. He didn't want to tell her. Why? "And the middleman would be…?"

"Of no interest to you," Nathan assured her.

"Nathan." There was a dangerous note in her voice. "Who is this 'mystery' person and why are you acting like a poor man's would-be espionage agent?"

Nathan surrendered, knowing he couldn't win. "The middle 'man' is your mother," he mumbled. "Satisfied?"

"My mother," Kennon repeated, stunned. "And Aunt Maizie? They talked? They actually talked?"

It didn't seem possible. Her mother never spoke to her aunt. And she definitely never sought Aunt Maizie out, on that Kennon was willing to stake her life. From what she and Nikki—her cousin and Maizie's only daughter—could piece together, it had something to do with the fact that Kennon's aunt had married her mother's brother, and her mother had not thought that Maizie was good enough for him.

Her mother was the only one who felt Maizie wasn't good enough. As for Kennon, she adored her aunt and had told Nikki more than once that she envied her cousin's relationship with such a forward-thinking woman.

"Anytime you want to trade, just let me know," Nikki had said to her. At the time Nikki was somewhat upset because she claimed that her mother was forever trying to play matchmaker and set her up with someone.

These days, Nikki was no longer complaining, especially since, according to what Kennon had heard, Aunt Maizie was the one who had set Nikki up with the sensitive, handsome hunk she had just recently married.

Kennon supposed that was one thing in her mother's favor. Ruth Connors Cassidy didn't play matchmaker, at least not anymore, she thought with a smile. Not since all the eligible sons of her mother's friends had been taken off the market.

But Aunt Maizie was making matches like gangbusters. What if her mother had gone to Aunt Maizie and asked her to…?

No. She was allowing her imagination to run away with her. Her mother wouldn't do that. Besides, she was through with men. To hell with all of them—except of course for Nathan, she amended. But then, he was more like a brother than a man anyway.

Kennon frowned into the small oval mirror over the pedestal sink. "Since I look like something that the cat dragged in, why don't you go in my place?" she suggested.

Nathan shook his head. "A, you no longer look like something that the cat dragged in. And B, the client said he only wanted to deal with the owner. In case your brain is still a little foggy, that would be you."

"Since you took the referral, what else do you know?" she asked him.

"Only that your aunt sold him the house and the man has no furniture. He wants you to furnish his house."

There was no point in fighting this, she thought. And maybe this was what she needed, a new project.

Decorating a whole house could come to a tidy little commission. "All right, get me the address and I'm on my way."

"Got it right here," Nathan told her, taking a folded piece of paper out of his vest pocket. "Printed out a map for you and everything," he added, opening up the paper and handing it to her with a flourish. "Since I know how GPS-challenged you are."

"I'm not GPS-challenged," she corrected him. "I just don't like a machine telling me where to go." Kennon looked at him pointedly. "I already get enough of that from you."

Nathan took no offense. "You know you love it."

"Keep reminding me," Kennon instructed wearily.

She was still thinking that long after Nathan's voice had faded away and she had made the quick seven-mile trip to her destination. Right now, she felt like thirty miles of bad road. The last thing she wanted to do was meet a new client. But the economy being what it was, no job was too small at this point. And Nathan did say the man wanted enough furniture to fill his whole house. Hopefully, the man was not living in a one-bedroom house.

Dear God, Kennon, where's your optimism? Where's your hope? How could you have let that creep get to you this way? Nathan's right. The breakup was a godsend. It saved you from making a stupid mistake. You didn't love Pete, you loved the idea of him. Now get over it, damn it!

Following Nathan's map, she made another turn to the right. A few yards from the corner stood a magnificent two-story house.

Getting out of her vehicle, Kennon didn't bother locking the door. She walked up to the huge front door and rang the bell. The next second, the beginning notes of the Anvil Chorus sounded throughout the house.

Well, at least it wasn't taps, she thought.

Chapter Two

Simon Sheffield frowned as he tried to hurry into his clothes. His alarm hadn't gone off. Or, if it had, he'd shut it off in his sleep, instinctively attempting to escape from the annoying sound.

Uneasiness arrived the moment he was awake. The same question he'd been grappling with for the last week assaulted him again. Had he made a colossal mistake by uprooting the girls and moving here?

But then, what choice had he had? Seeing all those familiar surroundings in San Francisco had slowly ripped him to pieces. The entire city was fraught with memories for him and while some people could take comfort in memories when they'd lost someone, Simon found himself haunted by them.

Haunted to the point that he was having trouble focusing in order to function properly. And focusing to the exclusion of everything else was crucial in his line of work.

Time and again he'd find himself frozen in a moment that whispered of Nancy and all the things they had once had, all the plans they had once made. Nancy, who was the light of not only his life but the lives of everyone she came in contact with. Nancy, who was the embodiment of optimism and hope, who could almost heal with the touch of her hand, the warmth of her smile. Nancy, for whom nothing was impossible.

Except coming back from the dead.

And she was dead because of him.

Dead because his urgent sense of duty and ethics had prevented him from keeping his prior promise to Doctors Without Borders. A much sought-after and gifted cardiovascular surgeon, Simon had willingly signed up to donate fifteen days of his service, going to a wretchedly impoverished region on the eastern coast of Africa. But when the time came for him to go, one of his patients, Jeremy Winterhaus, had suffered the collapse of one of the new valves that had been put in during his emergency bypass surgery. Always a man who saw things through, Simon hadn't felt comfortable about leaving Winterhaus in the care of another surgeon. Nancy, a general surgeon herself, had immediately stepped in and told him not to worry. She'd urged him to see to his patient, and she'd happily taken his place in the program.

And died in his place when the tsunami, born in the wake of the 8.3 earthquake that had ripped through Indonesia, swept away her and more than two dozen other people less than three days later.

Edna had been the one to break the news to him,

tapping on his door the morning that the tsunami had hit, her eyes red-rimmed from weeping. Edna O'Malley had once been Nancy's nanny and was now nanny to their two daughters, Madelyn and Meghan. She had come into his bedroom and in her soft, quiet voice said the words that ended the world as he knew it.

"Our Nancy was swept out to sea by a tsunami, Doctor."

He'd stared at her in disbelief, then felt as if he'd been repeatedly stabbed in the gut with a rusted serrated knife.

Thirteen months later, he still hadn't healed. He knew that if he had a prayer of moving forward and providing for their girls, he needed to start somewhere fresh and lock away all the memories until such time as it wouldn't hurt so much to be confronted by them.

Because of her ties to Nancy, he'd almost left Edna back in San Francisco, as well. But he needed someone to look after the girls while he was away at the hospital, someone he trusted. As a cardiovascular surgeon he couldn't lay claim to an average nine-to-five existence, and he needed someone to be there to fill in the gaps. Finding a new nanny was much too time-consuming.

Besides, Edna needed something to keep her going, as well, a reason for waking up in the morning. Simon was well aware that in her own way, Edna had loved Nancy as much as he did, as much as a mother did. And she loved the girls, as well. To lose all three of them in thirteen months would have destroyed the woman, and God knew he didn't want someone else on his conscience.

Simon felt he already had more than enough guilt to deal with.

He had to get moving, Simon upbraided himself. It

was late. Getting out of bed in the morning was still unbelievably difficult for him. Especially when, for just a glimmer of a moment, when he first opened his eyes in the morning, he didn't remember.

And then he did.

The full weight of remembering oppressed him to the point that he had trouble breathing. But it was slowly getting easier. Not easy, but just easier, and that, he knew, was all he could logically hope for.

If he was going to be of any use to his patients and the hospital where he would be working, Simon knew he needed to get back to the business of living.

Which was why being late for his first meeting with Dr. Edward Hale, the chief of surgery at Blair Memorial, was not a very good idea.

When the doorbell rang with its odd, teeth-jarring chimes, it was just one more thing for him to be annoyed about.

Now what? he wondered impatiently as he shrugged into his jacket. The obligatory necktie was stuffed into his pocket, knotted and ready to be pressed into service should he need it. As a rule, he hated ties and saw them as an unnecessary evil.

A sneeze in the distance told him that Edna was making her way to the front door. The last couple of days, she seemed to be coming down with a bad cold despite her protests that she was fine.

When it rained...

"I'll get it, Edna," he called out. Edna already had more than her hands full, Simon thought, just getting Madelyn, eight, and Meghan, six, ready for school.

But even though he'd just told her that he would open

the front door on his way out, he knew Edna was too stubborn to retreat.

Sure enough, there she was, hurrying to the door. Dedicated right down to the soles of her excessively sensible shoes, Edna O'Malley appeared a bit older than her sixty-seven years and was, to the undiscerning eye, the epitome of the comfortable, capable British nanny of decades past. Not exactly plump, but far from thin, at five foot ten Edna cast a considerable shadow.

"I'm not dead yet, Doctor," Edna told him firmly, refusing to tolerate being coddled in any manner. She struggled to stifle the deep cough that insisted on rumbling inside her chest.

Simon shook his head. "You will be if you don't take it easy," he warned her.

Edna spared him a reproving glance. "If that's the kind of medical advice you're dispensing, Doctor, it's a surprise to me there's no wolf at our door. But wait, perhaps that's him now," Edna amended glibly as she opened the massive door. Lights danced in through the beveled glass, casting multicolored bursts on the wall. "No, no wolf. A waif instead," the nanny pronounced after giving the slender young woman standing on their doorstep a quick once-over.

The next moment, Edna quickly turned her head toward the door and sneezed loudly enough to befit a person twice her size and girth.

"Bless you," Kennon said automatically. "I have an appointment to see a Dr. Simon Sheffield."

Edna sneezed a third time, sighed heavily as she dug into her deep pockets for her handkerchief and blew her nose before giving the young woman another critical once-over.

Sniffling, she wadded the handkerchief back up and shoved it into her pocket again. "I'm afraid the doctor doesn't do house calls, miss—even from his own house. You'll have to see him during office hours in his office."

Okay, this was obviously a misunderstanding. "But I'm not sick," Kennon began. She got no further.

"Good for you," the nanny declared. "That makes one of us. Me, I'm feeling rather poorly," she went on to confide as she lowered her voice.

Kennon tried to look sympathetic while wondering what any of this had to do with her appointment. She pressed her lips together. Had there been a mistake?

The next moment, before she could speak further to the sneezing woman who stood in her way, she caught a movement out of the corner of her eye.

A man, undoubtedly the poster boy for the description of "tall, dark and handsome," came to the door. In his wake came two very lively little girls, obviously his. Each had the man's bright blue eyes and thick hair, except that his was dark and theirs was a lighter shade of brown and curly. And, unlike their father, the little girls weren't scowling. They were just eyeing her curiously.

"Who's that, Daddy?" the younger one asked, staring up at her with the bluest eyes Kennon had ever seen.

"A lady who's selling something," he assumed. With a careful movement, he edged both Edna and his daughters back behind him and stood facing the woman on his doorstep. Attractive though she was, whatever the woman was selling, he had no time to hear her sales pitch. "I'm sorry but I'm in a hurry," he apologized politely, "and I don't have time to buy anything."

"I wasn't planning on pressuring you into buying

anything in five minutes flat," Kennon assured the good-looking physician.

Furnishing a house took time and while she always accompanied a client when he or she went out to purchase an item, even subtly guiding them toward certain things, the ultimate choice was always theirs. After all, they were the ones who had to live with whatever they wound up selecting.

Kennon wasn't prepared for the puzzled, somewhat annoyed look that came over the man's face.

The woman *was* trying to sell him something. Subscriptions? he guessed, glancing at the rather large, square briefcase in her hand.

Or did she represent some pharmaceutical company, wanting to snare his attention before any of the others got to him? He knew all about how competitive sales reps could be, but until now, he'd always had someone shielding him. One of the receptionists or office managers would field the calls, make appropriate comments and promise that "someone" would be getting back to them.

Had they taken to trying to corner physicians before they got to the office? It seemed unusual, but not out of the question. Competition, he'd heard, was steep and cutthroat.

Obviously, they'd sent their most attractive saleswoman. He couldn't help wondering if she had a brain, as well, or if chutzpa was all she was gifted with. That and possibly the longest legs he'd ever seen.

"Wow," he murmured, "and I thought that the companies in San Francisco were pushy."

"That's just the point, Doctor. I'm *not* pushy," Kennon quietly corrected him. "The ultimate choice in what you decide to buy or not buy is yours. All I do is just make a variety of suggestions."

She had, he thought, the closest thing to a perfect figure he'd ever seen. But it still wasn't enough to make him promise to advise his patients to take one drug above another, just because *her* packaging was better than some other company's. He had to believe in a medication before he prescribed it.

He needed to get this woman out of here—and himself, as well. Suppressing a few exasperated words that rose to his lips, Simon took hold of the petite blonde's arm and firmly moved her across the threshold, back to his doorstep. "Look, I'm sure whatever you're pushing has a market, but right now, I'm not interested."

Aunt Maizie, you're really going to have to test these guys for sanity before you send them on to someone, Kennon thought.

She saw the man's little girls standing directly behind him, their blue eyes as big as proverbial saucers as they peered out at her. The little one smiled shyly at her.

The girls were adorable. Hopefully for their sake they were adopted, since insanity could run in the family, she thought.

Kennon glanced back at the doctor. "Look, Dr. Sheffield, I can't just do this hit-and-run. You're obviously too busy right now and I need some time in order to do my job properly." He stared at her as if she'd suddenly started speaking pig Latin, so she tried to make him understand her approach. "I usually try to get to know a few things about my client before I really get started."

The man still appeared stunned, not to mention somewhat bemused.

"It's very important to me that you wind up liking

what I do, not just for a referral for future jobs, but because I like leaving satisfied clients in my wake."

He'd heard that drug reps were pushy, getting information about doctors so they could appeal to them on a friendly level, approach them like old friends instead of potential markets for their employer's product. This one was in a class by herself. He was almost tempted to ask her who she represented, but that would only be opening the door for her and he had a feeling that she could go on and on.

"I really don't have time for this."

Kennon looked past the doctor's rather broad shoulders and into the heart of the house. It was a beautiful house. Beautiful and barren. He really did need some furniture. If only to give his daughters a feeling of stability.

"But your house is empty," she protested. "You need furniture."

"What does that have to do with it?" he asked.

"Everything," Kennon insisted. Okay, maybe she should start all over again, she told herself. She'd obviously lost the man somewhere. "I'm Kennon Cassidy." She put her hand out. When he didn't take it immediately, she added, "The decorator." She waited for the light to dawn in his incredibly beautiful, piercing blue eyes. It didn't. Maybe the man had a short attention span and needed more input. "Maizie Sommers told you I'd be coming." She took a breath. Still nothing. She added a coda. "She said you had an empty house that was badly in need of furnishing."

That was when the bells finally went off in his head. "Oh. Maizie," he repeated, recalling the savvy, attractive woman who had helped him find what she'd referred to as "the right house for your girls." He'd been completely at a loss when he'd gone to the Realtor. She'd all but reshaped him with her bare hands. For a moment he clung to the familiar name like a drowning man clung to a life preserver that had suddenly drifted within his reach.

Simon nodded, feeling more than a little like a fool for having made the mistake. If he'd let her talk instead of cutting her off at every sentence, maybe this misunderstanding wouldn't have taken up so much time.

He intended to make it up to her by giving her decorative services a try. But right now, he had someplace he needed to be. A cardiovascular surgeon wasn't much good to anyone if he didn't have the backing of an accredited hospital where he was allowed to perform his surgeries.

"I'm afraid that I'm going to have to reschedule our meeting. I have another one to go to right now at Blair Memorial Hospital." He felt after everything that had just gone down, he owed her a little bit of an explanation. "I've been invited to join the hospital's staff, but I have a feeling that if I don't show up for my first meeting with the chief of surgery, that invitation just might be rescinded."

Now, that at least was beginning to make sense. Kennon nodded.

"Of course. I understand completely. I run into time conflicts all the time." Opening her purse, she riffled through a few things in her wallet before finding her card. She handed it to him. "Feel free to call me whenever you find you have the time to reschedule. If I'm not in the office, the call will be forwarded to either my cell or my home phone, depending on where I am."

Simon closed his hand over the card. The corners of his generous mouth curved ever so slightly. "Thanks for being understanding about this," he apologized. "Things have been up in the air lately and we've just relocated to the area—"

Kennon nodded, wanting to spare him having to go over things needlessly. "No need to explain, Dr. Sheffield. My aunt filled me in on the details."

Simon eyed her a little uncertainly. "Your aunt?"

Her smile swiftly traveled into her eyes. "The woman who showed you the house you just bought," she prompted.

After Nathan had told her that her aunt had actually made the appointment for the client, Kennon made it a point to call her as she drove to the Newport Beach house. She never liked walking into something completely unprepared, so she had called Maizie and asked for background information on the client.

Maizie had told her that the man was a surgeon and that he had two small daughters, Madelyn and Meghan. She'd also mentioned that he'd moved here from San Francisco. As a P.S. she'd thrown in at the end that he was a widower. What her aunt had neglected to tell her, Kennon thought, was that he was breathtakingly good-looking.

Aunt Maizie probably thought that was the cherry on the sundae, Kennon reasoned.

Poor Aunt Maizie didn't know about the new leaf that Pete had made her turn. She was no longer in the market for anything but peace and quiet. Men did not fit under that heading. Not in any manner, shape or form. Ergo, she was no longer in the market for one.

"Oh," Simon was saying. "You aunt is a very nice woman."

He'd get no argument from her. "Yes, she is," Kennon agreed.

From behind him the nanny's rather reedy voice called out to him. "Dr. Sheffield."

"Just a minute, Mrs. O'Malley," he responded formally without turning in the woman's direction. "Again, I just wanted to explain that it was an honest mistake. I'm told that sales reps for pharmaceutical companies can be very devious and almost ruthless—"

She picked up the cue. "And you think I'm devious and ruthless?" she asked, tongue in cheek.

Cut from a serious cloth these days, Simon didn't realize she was kidding and instantly protested. "I didn't mean to imply that I thought you were, I mean—" He was tripping over his own tongue, trying to apologize for the insult he hadn't actually given.

Kennon was more than happy to absolve him of blame and free him from the awkward moment. She laughed lightly, feeling sorry for the man's distress. Who would have thought that anyone this handsome could also know how to apologize.

"Please, Doctor, don't give it another thought."

"Dr. Sheffield," Edna called again. This time her voice was even reedier than before. It broke and faded toward the end.

And then there was a loud thud, as if a large suitcase had been dropped on the floor. At the same moment, Madelyn, his eight-year-old, suddenly screamed and cried out, "Daddy!" in a frightened, high-pitched voice.

Swinging around, Simon saw that his children's nanny was lying facedown and prone on the floor.

"Hurry!" Madelyn implored, frantically beckoning him over with both hands. "Hurry, Daddy," she said again. "Edna's dead!"

Beside her, Meghan covered her eyes and began to scream. Loudly.

Chapter Three

Whirling around, Simon immediately hurried over to the fallen nanny. Crouching over Edna, he checked her pulse and was relieved with his findings. The pulse was going fast, but it was strong.

"She's not dead, Madelyn," he told his daughter, indicating Edna's chest area, which was rising and falling rhythmically.

Nonetheless, Madelyn didn't appear to be completely convinced. "Then why are her eyes closed?"

"'Cause she's sleeping." Meghan emphasized the last word with feeling. She looked at her sister as if Madelyn should have known that.

"That's not a bad explanation," Simon observed, surprised with his younger daughter's assessment. Meghan took it as praise and preened before her sister.

Other than a few words of greeting each day, Simon hadn't been accustomed to actually talking with his daughters. That had been a domain reserved for Nancy. Since her death, he'd found himself in a whole new world with little to no clue on how to navigate in it. Children were for the most part a mysterious breed to him.

Aware that both his daughters were looking at him expectantly, he explained, "Edna fainted. She hasn't been feeling well these last couple of days and she probably just turned too quickly." He'd been too busy getting ready this morning to notice, but now that he reflected, Edna had been coughing and sneezing a great deal more today than yesterday.

Madelyn still didn't look convinced, or at ease. Her eyes still wide, she asked her father in a halting voice, "Is she— Is Edna going to be all right?" She stood there, nervously waiting for an answer. "She's not going to— well, you know." She lifted her small shoulders, as if the word on her tongue was too heavy to bear or utter. "Like Mama," she finally whispered, trusting her father to make the connection.

He'd been desperately trying to put a lid on his grief this past year, but he hadn't been oblivious. He had noticed that of his two daughters, Nancy's death seemed to have affected Madelyn more than it had Meghan. The latter had cried when she'd been told, but she also recovered a great deal sooner than Madelyn had, transferring her affection and loyalty to Edna almost effortlessly.

But then, Meghan was only six and she hadn't realized yet just how hard life could knock you down when you were least expecting it.

"Is there anything I can do to help?" the soft voice behind him asked.

Simon realized that he'd all but forgotten about the

decorator. Probably the first man who ever had, he judged, given how attractive she was.

"Yes, you can hold the girls back," he instructed. He didn't want either of them getting underfoot, even if it was eagerness to help that propelled them.

Scooping the unconscious nanny up into his arms, Simon struggled to his feet.

Edna was a decidedly solid woman, he thought, as his arms strained and a rather odd pain cut across the tops of his thighs. The woman was strong for her age. The downside of that was she was also heavy.

As she heard him take a deep breath that suggested he was glad he'd risen without embarrassing himself, Kennon watched the man in silent amazement. Not many men could have done that so smoothly. Ordinarily, they would have either left the woman on the floor until she regained consciousness or asked for help in getting her up and onto a more comfortable surface. He'd just squatted and had done what amounted to a dead lift, an exercise favored by dedicated bodybuilders.

Kennon continued to keep a light but restraining hand on each of the girls' shoulders, holding them back until their father began to walk. And then, still resting a hand on each of their shoulders, she gently guided Madelyn and Meghan into the living room, behind their father.

It was then that she noticed that the doctor actually did have one piece of furniture downstairs—a sofa that appeared completely out of place in the wide, cathedral-ceilinged room. The maroon, oversize sofa was sagging in a number of places and definitely did not look as if it belonged in the house.

A loaner?

She remembered that on occasion her aunt would

make use of one of those companies that rented furniture out by the month. She did it to give the property she was showing a warmer look. Obviously that hadn't been the goal here. Rather than bright and cheery, the sofa just looked worn and ready to be retired.

Still, it had to be more comfortable than the floor, she reasoned. And the object here was Edna's comfort, even if she was still unconscious.

Troubled, shifting from foot to foot, Madelyn gave no indication that she'd been placated by her father's answer. "Are you sure she's not dead?" the eight-year-old asked anxiously.

Kennon smiled into Madelyn's face, fielding the question for him. "Your father's a doctor, honey. I'm sure he knows the difference between someone being dead or alive. Besides—" she leaned in closer to the girl "—if you look very carefully, you can see Edna's chest rising and falling. That means she's breathing. Breathing is a very good indication that your nanny's alive."

With a sniff that told Kennon Madelyn was doing her best not to cry, the little girl solemnly nodded her head. "Okay," she said, accepting the explanation. Even so, her eyes were shining with unshed tears. "It's just that Mama—"

"Never mind," her father said, cutting her off briskly. He had no desire to have his personal life spread out before a total stranger. Turning from the sofa, he looked at the decorator his Realtor had sent. She seemed at ease, standing between his daughters like that, he noted. Something he hadn't quite been able to manage yet. "Miss—" He stopped short, realizing that he was missing a crucial piece of information. "What did you say your name was?"

"Cassidy. Kennon," she added, supplying her first name without being asked. She smiled at the girls. "I know it's not the easiest name to remember."

The doctor frowned slightly, or was that his normal expression, Kennon wondered. If it was, it was a shame, because he was too good-looking a man to detract from his features by perpetually frowning.

"Ease is not always of tantamount importance," the doctor told her. "But manners are."

He was a disciplinarian, Kennon guessed. She wondered if he realized how hard that could be on his daughters.

Her own father had been a Marine colonel who lived and breathed the service long after he retired from it. He was quite possibly the most distant man she'd ever known. Growing up with him had been like growing up with a disapproving stranger. Maybe it was her need for acceptance and affection that had made her pick the wrong man to love in the first place.

She heard Simon sigh in obvious exasperation.

Kennon's attention was immediately drawn to the woman on the sofa. "Is something wrong?"

Simon's frown deepened. "You mean other than the fact that I need to be at a meeting at the hospital with the chief of surgery in less than half an hour, my girls are due in school and my housekeeper is ill and presently unconscious?" he asked with barely suppressed sarcasm. "No, nothing's wrong."

Well, that tongue of his wasn't about to melt butter anytime soon, Kennon thought. Still, with all that on his plate, she supposed she couldn't really fault his less than sunny disposition. A lot of men were lost without their wives and he was one of them. She found that oddly appealing.

"You wouldn't happen to know where I could find a capable young woman to take my daughters to school and then come back to keep an eye on my housekeeper until I can come home, would you?" His tone indicated that he wasn't actually expecting an answer. He was just blowing off a little steam as he searched for a solution to his overwhelming dilemma.

Kennon paused for a moment. She had cleared her entire morning to give Dr. Sheffield the proper amount of time for a first decorator-client meeting. She wasn't due anywhere, which meant that she was free to ride to his rescue. Ordinarily, she wouldn't hesitate, but this situation was a little different.

Kennon couldn't quite make up her mind whether she thought of Simon Sheffield as exceedingly businesslike or a martinet just this side of stuffy and rude. But she'd always had a soft spot when it came to children, and his daughters were adorable. The man was obviously in need of help. If she came to his aid, maybe the man would feel obligated to engage her services and hire her to decorate his house.

No, she reconsidered, he didn't strike her as the type who felt obligated or believed in the eye-for-an-eye theory. Not unless it involved pistols at ten paces.

Still, he did need help, she did have the time and she had an affinity for children. She'd always had a weakness for the short set, Kennon thought fondly. And it was obvious to everyone. An only child, she'd started babysitting at a young age and had loved kids as far back as she could remember.

Her mother frequently told her that she had the

makings of a wonderful mother. This observation was *always* accompanied by a plaintive lament that it was such a shame that she hadn't started a family yet.

Maybe someday. And if her "clock" ran out as she waited for "someday" to come, adoption for single mothers was getting easier.

Oh, what the hell? What did she have to lose by volunteering? Kennon made up her mind.

"Me," she said.

There was confusion in his deep blue eyes. "You what?"

"The capable person you're looking for," Kennon told him. "I can be her. I mean, I *am* her." What *was* it about this man that made her talk as if she had a speech impediment? Kennon blew out a breath and started from the top again. "I can take your girls to school if you tell me which school they're attending, and then I can come back and stay with your housekeeper until you get back." The doctor didn't appear to be won over by her proposal. "If you're worried about Mrs. O'Malley being alone while I take the girls, I can call my assistant. Nathan will stay with her until I get back."

"Why?" Simon asked, not attempting to hide the fact that he was scrutinizing her as he asked. He might have gotten along well with her father. Too bad her dad hadn't stayed in touch after her parents divorced.

Kennon wasn't sure exactly what Simon was asking. She had volunteered a lot of information just now. "Excuse me?"

"Why would you do that?" he asked her. "Take my daughters to school and have your assistant babysit Edna?" Where he came from, people kept to themselves, they didn't volunteer to help, especially not essential strangers.

He certainly was the uptight, suspicious type. She was really beginning to feel sorry for his daughters. "Because you just said—"

He waved his hand at her explanation, dismissing it. "I know what I just said, but we're strangers."

Was that it? She laughed. "Not for long if I'm going to decorate your house." She'd already told him that she needed to get to know him in order to do her job—or hadn't he been paying attention at all? "I can't think of a better way to get to know you, Dr. Sheffield, than jumping feet first into your life."

The image obviously captivated the younger of his two daughters. Meghan started giggling. "Can I watch you jump?" she asked.

Kennon couldn't resist running her hand along the little girl's soft cheek. Meghan was nothing if not adorably squeezable, but she refrained, knowing from first-hand experience and her mother's annoying great-aunt, that children didn't like being squeezed.

"It's just an expression, honey," Kennon told her with a laugh. Then she looked at Simon, still waiting for his response. "Offer's still open."

He was not in a position to be picky and he supposed that if this overly friendly decorator came with the real-estate woman's recommendation—Maizie Sommers had reminded him of his own late mother—at least that was better than finding someone in the classified section and taking his chances.

Resigned—his back was up against the wall—he nodded and took out his house key. He held it out to the decorator—he'd forgotten her name again. "Thanks. I appreciate this. By the way, there's no need to call in your assistant."

He almost sounded as if he meant what he said about thanking her, she thought. Of course, it might have helped if he'd smiled when he said it, but she had a feeling that Simon Sheffield didn't do much smiling. Pocketing the key, she asked an all-important question. "And the name of their school?" she asked him.

"Saint Elizabeth Ann Seton," Edna murmured weakly.

"Edna, you *are* alive!" Madelyn cried, overjoyed. She threw her arms around the woman, giving her a fierce hug. Meghan piled on top of her.

"Let her breathe, girls," Simon warned sternly. The next moment he moved his daughters back, away from their nanny. "How are you feeling?" he asked the woman. He took her pulse again. It was still rapid, but not as reedy as it'd been. The beat was stronger now.

"Embarrassed," Edna replied in a voice that still had very little strength behind it.

"Nothing to be embarrassed about," he dismissed crisply. "I want you to rest here for at least a few hours— until I get back."

Edna looked dismayed. She tried to sit up, but was too weak for the moment to follow through. "But the girls—" she began to protest.

"Are being taken care of," Simon assured the nanny. He turned to the woman who seemed to be a godsend— if he actually believed in things like that. "The girls' school is on—"

Kennon held up her hand to stop him. "I grew up here," she told him. "I know where Saint Elizabeth Ann Seton School is." She began to usher the girls toward the front door. "By the way, the hospital you're going to, you said that it was Blair Memorial—"

"Yes," he cut in suspiciously. "Why?"

Definitely not the most trusting of men, she thought. Did the distrust come naturally to him, or had something caused it, she wondered.

"Nothing. I just wanted to say that Blair has a great reputation. My cousin is a pediatrician and she's affiliated with Blair. Dr. Nicole Connors," she supplied. She saw him raise a brow at the surname. "As it happens, she's your real-estate agent's daughter." The moment she filled him in, she could guess at his next thought. "Yes, it really is a small world around here." She turned her attention back to her temporary charges. "Okay, girls, we need to hustle if we're going to get you to the school before lunch."

"Lunch?" Madelyn cried, clearly dismayed. "Are we that late?"

Okay, she was going to have to tone down her humor, Kennon thought.

"Just another figure of speech," she explained. With a hand once more on each girl's shoulder, she ushered Madelyn and Meghan out the door. And then she looked over her shoulder at the doctor before hurrying off to her vehicle. "I'll be back as soon as I can," she promised in case he thought she was going to dawdle before returning to the nanny.

Simon nodded. "So will I," he replied.

As the woman with the rapid-fire mouth left, closing the door behind her, Simon had the unshakable impression that he had just been in the company of a grade-five hurricane.

But at least he was still standing, he told himself, and that had to be worth something.

Blair Memorial Hospital was absolutely everything he'd been led to believe it was when he had first gotten in contact with Dr. Edward Hale. First-rate in all fields, it was state-of-the-art when it came to cardiac surgery. The hospital even boasted of having a Gamma Knife available. A Gamma Knife afforded surgeons a virtually unobtrusive method of operating that their brethren of the last century could have only dreamed about. For the most part, it had been regarded as science fiction—until it crossed over and became real.

At one point not that long ago, Simon would have gotten very excited about the possibilities that lay ahead of him. Except that these days he felt exceedingly guilty about allowing himself to feel anything but a profound sense of loss and sadness.

Nancy wouldn't have wanted you to feel that way, the voice in his head insisted. The voice sounded a great deal like Edna at the moment because the woman had known his wife almost better than he had.

He knew that the voice—and Edna—were probably right. Nancy would have wanted him to move on. But he couldn't. His body, his entire psyche felt as if it was stuck in molasses, in the past, unable to move, unable to blink. Unable to think of life without his partner, his helper, his soul mate.

Remember the girls. They need you.

This time, the voice in his head sounded a great deal like Nancy.

He realized that the chief of surgery was shaking his

hand, a pleased expression on the older man's broad, kind face.

"Well, I've got nothing further to say right now except welcome aboard, Doctor," he told Simon. Eminently satisfied, the older man added, "I think this is the beginning of a beautiful friendship." Flashing an almost perfect set of teeth, he identified the quote. "That's from *Casablanca*. You'll forgive me, I'm a big movie buff. My wife, bless her, has another term for it, but I like *movie buff* better. Wives, God love 'em, they've all got our number, don't they?"

Hale chuckled as he looked at the face of Blair's newest surgeon on staff. And then the chief of surgery suddenly grew somber.

"Oh, my God, I'm sorry. I forgot that your wife passed," he said delicately, falling back on the squeaky-clean euphemism for death. "I'm sorry, Doctor. That had to have sounded very callous of me."

Simon shook his head, doing his very best to detach his consciousness from his surroundings. He'd been doing that for a year now, whenever his thoughts or the conversation veered toward Nancy.

"No, that's all right," he demurred, hoping the matter would be dropped.

Not likely. Hale didn't appear to be finished just yet. Concerned, he laid his hand on Simon's shoulder and peered into the other man's eyes.

"How are you getting along?" Hale asked, adding kindly, "Do you need anything?"

Yes, I need my wife back.

Stoically, Simon shook his head. "No, I'm fine. But that's very kind of you." Simon glanced at his watch. Three hours had gone by. Had the meeting taken that long? He didn't feel as if it had, but it obviously must have. "If you don't mind, my housekeeper's ill and I'd like to check in on her."

"Of course, of course." Hale rose, pumping Simon's hand again. "Let me know if there's anything we can do for you here at Blair Memorial. Otherwise, we'll be looking forward to seeing you at the hospital, say, on Thursday?" he suggested hopefully. He knew that most places began their people on a Monday, but he had another philosophy. "We'll let you get your feet wet slowly," he added with a chuckle. "I always found that was the best way. I don't like overwhelming my doctors by having them start with a full week. Even a state-of-the-art hospital takes some getting used to," he theorized.

"Thursday will be fine."

"Remember," Hale said, walking Simon to the glass-paneled door, "if you find you need anything, or just want someone to talk to, please don't hesitate to give me a call. My door—and phone—are always open." He clapped the new surgeon on the back. "I operate by a simple rule—Happy doctors are good doctors. I want to keep you happy, Dr. Sheffield."

"I appreciate that, chief." *But you're thirteen months too late for that.* "Thank you again, sir." And with that, Simon took his leave.

The second he turned down the corridor, Simon picked up speed.

He needed to get home to make sure that Edna was all right and that he hadn't made a huge mistake by opening his doors to that decorator.

Granted that this Kennon Cassidy did seem to have an engaging manner about her, but from what he'd heard, so did the more successful con artists. Although he had nothing in the house that could be taken, still he would feel a great deal more at ease once he was back, attending to Edna himself.

And reclaiming his solitude.

Chapter Four

Even though he had traveled behind the woman's vehicle for part of the way to Saint Elizabeth Ann Seton School and had subsequently called the principal, Sister Therese, to make sure that his daughters had arrived and each was in her proper classroom, the bottom line was that Simon was more than a little annoyed with himself for having actually relied on a woman he really didn't know from Adam.

Well, maybe not Adam, he amended. *Didn't know from Eve* would have been the more appropriate description, given that no one in their right mind would ever mistake Kennon Cassidy for anything but an exquisite example of womanhood.

His observation caught him off guard, completely surprising him. Where had that come from?

Ever since the tsunami had taken Nancy and swept

away his life, he'd caught himself sleepwalking through his life on more than one occasion.

He needed to maintain a grip on his life.

If he didn't, he wouldn't be any good to anyone, least of all himself. And there were not just his patients—his future patients—to think of, but his daughters, as well.

He'd been an absentee father at best, but it had never preyed on his conscience because Nancy and especially Edna were there to take up the slack. Nancy's death had changed all the ground rules. He had to ante up, despite the fact that he didn't know how.

It was for Madelyn and Meghan's sake that he had deliberately left everything behind and come here in an attempt to finally shake free of the malaise that Nancy's death had created. And to some extent, he had succeeded. He'd applied for a position at the hospital, actually bought a home in an amazingly short amount of time and had gotten the girls enrolled in a top-ranked school, although the last was more Edna's doing than his own.

But if someone were to ask him what color his shirt was, or to even hazard a guess as to what either of his daughters was wearing this morning, he'd have no answer. For the most part, he'd always been rather unaware of his surroundings, but it had only gotten worse in the last thirteen months.

So he was rather stunned he'd actually noticed what could politely be referred to as Kennon Cassidy's "attributes."

He supposed that just meant he wasn't dead yet. Maybe that represented a sliver of hope that he would eventually be able to come around—in about a thousand years or so.

* * *

When he took the freeway off-ramp that would eventually lead him to his house, Simon glanced at the clock on the dashboard. It had taken him less time to drive back than it had to reach the hospital. The realization meant that his subconscious was apparently back online. He had always had the ability to commit things to memory after seeing them only once. This included driving directions. But even that had been less than fully operational these last thirteen months.

Pulling up into his driveway, Simon noted that the decorator—Kennon, was it?—had parked her pearl-blue sedan at the curb. She'd come back after dropping off the girls, just as she'd promised.

All right, so he'd lucked out. She'd kept her word. He still shouldn't have trusted her so readily, he silently lectured himself. With his dry cleaning, maybe, but not his daughters. What had he been thinking?

That was the problem; he hadn't been. All he knew was that he couldn't cancel his meeting. First impressions were infinitely important. There were no "do overs."

In his own defense, Simon thought, getting out of his car, the woman had come recommended and his back had been against the proverbial wall….

Simon cut himself a little slack.

The second he unlocked the front door and walked in, he became aware of it. It was impossible not to be. The aroma embraced him like a warm hug. For a moment, he stopped to inhale deeply and savor it. Then he began to walk briskly, following the enticing aroma to its source, the kitchen.

But to get to the kitchen, he had to walk through the

living room. Edna, he found, was still there. But now her head rested on a pillow and a crisp, light blue fleece blanket was spread over two thirds of her torso.

She looked better, he thought. He was relieved to see color in her cheeks and that she appeared to be fully conscious and lucid. Edna smiled at him as he walked over to her.

"How are you feeling, Edna?" he wanted to know.

"Much better now, thank you, Doctor." The color in her cheeks deepened as a touch of embarrassment passed over them. "I'm sorry I created such a fuss," she apologized, then confided, "It's the first time I've fainted since I was a young girl, and we all know how long ago that was."

The woman didn't have a vain bone in her body, but every woman needed to be reassured that she was attractive, he thought. Nancy had taught him that.

Simon took one of his housekeeper's weathered, capable hands in his own. "Not that long ago," he contradicted. Simon had examined Edna and satisfied himself that her fainting episode had been brought on by her cold, coupled with dehydration due to her failure to replenish the lost fluids. In other words, Edna was being typically Edna and neglecting to take the time to take care of herself. A little bed rest, as well as drinking plenty of liquids, and he was confident that she would be back to her old self in no time. "And I'm sorry I had to leave you alone like that—"

"It couldn't be helped, sir. I quite understand. And you didn't leave me alone," Edna pointed out politely. "That very lovely young woman came back after taking the girls to school. Been fussing over me as if I was a blood relative of hers since she returned." Edna shook her head in amazement. "She insisted on making me 'comfortable,' by bringing down some of my bedding." She nodded toward the sheet. "And she's in the kitchen right now, making some chicken soup for me to eat." Edna smiled. It was obvious that she was enjoying this. "She's a rare one, she is, sir."

Simon glanced in the direction of the kitchen. The aroma grew stronger, more enticing. Or was that because he was hungry?

"You mean she's heating up a can of soup." Since he'd donated their microwave to charity and had yet to purchase a replacement down here, he assumed that the decorator had emptied the contents of a store-bought can of soup into a saucepan and was in the process of heating it up now, hence the aroma.

"No, I mean she's making it," Edna insisted, coughing at the end of her sentence. After a moment, Edna regrouped and continued, her words coming out in a more measured cadence, as if she was fearful of irritating her throat. "She came in with a whole bag of groceries stuffed with all the ingredients to make an old-fashioned bowl of chicken soup. Heard her chopping celery and carrots like a pro," she related to him, approval wrapped around each word. "I thought all the girls her age just assumed that soup came from a can." Edna told him. And then she smiled.

"I'm feeling better just smelling it. Reminds me of home when I was a little girl. Mother always made me chicken soup whenever I was sick. Claimed it had healing properties. Whether it did or not I wouldn't be able to say, but everyone always felt better after Mother made chicken soup."

"Except the chicken," Simon speculated dryly.

"Maybe I'd better see what this decorator's up to," he decided out loud.

It wasn't that he wasn't grateful for the woman's efforts, especially for the way she had just pitched right in, doing whatever needed to be done for his daughters and for Edna, but he really just wanted to be alone, to feel that he had the house to himself. Granted, Edna was here, but Edna was always around and he regarded her much the way he did the air and the warmth of the sun, undemanding integrals of his life.

He had no desire to be put in a position where he had to carry on a conversation beyond a few necessary words. With the girls in school and Edna apparently feeling better, all he wanted to do was to entertain silence until such time that he had to go pick up the girls again.

With Kennon here that wasn't possible.

Standing in the doorway, he observed this invading woman for a couple of beats. And came to the conclusion that she looked more at home here than he did.

"Why are you making chicken soup?" he asked her without any sort of preamble.

Lost in thought, Kennon felt her heart suddenly lunge and get all but stuck in her throat. He'd startled her. Kennon tried her best not to show it.

"Because it won't make itself," she answered glibly, then gave him the real reason. "I always find that sipping soup when I'm coming down with a cold makes me feel better. Turns out that Edna feels the same way."

That still didn't explain why she'd felt compelled to make the damn thing from scratch. "Supermarkets have whole aisles devoted to chicken soup."

He saw her wrinkle her nose. It made her look intriguing—and rather cute.

"Chicken soup in cans," she pronounced disdainfully. "Not the same thing."

Coming closer, Simon glanced over her shoulder to see what she was actually stirring. He saw carrot shavings on the cutting board as well as an opened wrapper that told him she'd pressed a whole chicken into service for this undertaking. These ingredients didn't just magically appear.

"We didn't have any of this in the refrigerator," he said, indicating the wrapper and the carrot shavings. He knew that for a fact. He'd opened the refrigerator this morning, looking for the tin of coffee in order to properly kick-start a day that had already promised to go badly. The only thing in the refrigerator besides coffee, and milk for the girls, was one leftover container of Chinese food from last night's take-out dinner.

"Yes, I know," she told him, opening a drawer as she searched for a spoon. It took her two more tries before she located any silverware. She needed to sample the results of her efforts. Salting the soup was always tricky. She didn't want it to be bland, but she definitely didn't want it to be oversalted, either.

"You bought all this?" It was a rhetorical question, but he was nonetheless surprised.

She nodded, stirring the contents a little more. "It seemed easier than waiting for the supermarket fairy to make a drop."

He made no comment, other than to think that she obviously favored sarcasm. He took out his wallet and pulled out several bills. "How much do I owe you?"

The ingredients had cost her little. She could certainly

afford to spring for the tab. She waved her hand at his question.

"Why don't we see if Edna likes the soup first before we talk about owing anything," she suggested.

Opening the cupboard to the right of the stove, she found it all but bare. There were four dinner plates, four cups and four bowls all huddled together like the weary survivors of a shipwreck. Beyond that, there was nothing in the cupboards, not even dust.

"How long ago did you move in?" she asked him as she took down a bowl.

"A week ago," he told her, dispensing the information rather grudgingly.

"Well, that explains why the house is so barren." She placed the bowl on the counter beside the pot she was using. "How long before the moving van is supposed to get here?"

This was exactly what he hadn't wanted. A conversation. Other than being completely rude and ignoring her, he saw no option open to him but to answer her question.

"It isn't."

She looked at him, confused. She couldn't have heard right. "Excuse me?"

"There's no moving van," he said stoically. "At least not in the sense you mean. Some of the girls' things are being shipped out and Edna has some things coming, as well."

When he had first mentioned leaving everything behind, putting a few things in storage while donating the rest of the things to charities, the girls had been so upset he'd given in. But if he'd had his way, everything that reminded him of Nancy would be gone, or at the very least, stored out of sight until he could handle the memories. And the sorrow.

"The furniture is all going to be brand-new," he informed her. "Which is where you come in."

"If you don't mind my asking, did you have a fire?" Kennon asked.

His face appeared to close down. "No," he replied flatly, "I didn't."

If she was going to be of any use to this man, she needed to have the avenue of communication open, not sealed. He needed to *talk* to her.

"Then why—"

"And I do mind your asking," he told her, answering what she'd assumed was the rhetorical portion of her question.

It took Kennon a second to collect herself. "Okay. Then I won't ask," Kennon replied gamely, moving on. "When are you free?"

It was his turn to look at her blankly. Just what was the woman asking him? "For what?"

"To come shopping with me." She held her breath, waiting. Nothing was going to be easy with this man, was it?

He looked at her as if she'd just suggested that he go out for a run over hot coals while barefoot. "I'm not going shopping."

"All right, then I'm going to have to ask you some questions." *A lot of questions.* She resigned herself to the fact that it would probably be like pulling teeth. "Not about what happened to your things," she clarified quickly in response to the sharp look he sent her way. "But about your tastes, what you have in mind, how you see a particular room, like, let's say the family room."

"I see it as empty," he told her flatly. "I want to see it filled." That wasn't strictly true, so he amended his statement. "Actually, the girls and Edna want to have the rooms furnished. As for me, I don't care," his tone was devoid of any emotion, any feeling. "All I require is a bed, a table and some illumination at night in case I have some reading to do."

She stared at him for a moment, the spoon she was using to stir the soup suddenly frozen in midmovement. He was serious, wasn't he? "And nothing else? No sixty-inch HDTV set? No entertainment unit?"

Things like that had never been important to him. "No."

She laughed softly in disbelief. "I'm surprised some museum hasn't snatched you up and placed you under glass for viewing by the public. I've known men who've had to have their remote control surgically removed from their hand."

When Nancy and he had been dating, he could remember the two of them curling up on a sagging sofa, watching TV together. He'd done it mainly because Nancy enjoyed the programs. Since she was gone, he'd lost all interest in being vicariously entertained. Occasionally, one of the girls would drag him over to the set and attempt to get him to watch a show. He'd pretend to watch because it obviously meant something to his daughters, but usually his mind was far away. If anything, it was his work that grounded him. His work and his obligation to his daughters.

Pressing the dinner plate into service as a large saucer, Kennon placed the bowl onto it and then gingerly carried it out of the kitchen to the living room, where Edna sat, waiting.

"Are you going to give me any hints as to what you want?" she asked the doctor before she reached the older woman.

"For you to do your job," he replied simply. He saw the skeptical look in her eyes. "I promise I won't be difficult to please."

Too late for that, though she decided that it was wiser to keep the comment to herself. She did, however, want to set him straight about the job that was before her.

"Without a hint as to what direction your tastes run— country, modern, French provincial, eclectic, et cetera— my job is going to be pretty difficult."

"I thought this was what decorators dreamed of, a client who gives them free rein to do what they want."

The homes she decorated were extensions of her clients, not of herself.

"I have nothing to prove, Doctor, no ego to feed. My main objective is to please the clients, to have them walk into their house and feel as if they'd entered not just their sanctuary but their dream home. I can't succeed in creating that kind of feeling unless I know exactly what you'd like—and what you *don't* like," she emphasized.

He came to the only conclusion he could from her statement. "So you're turning down the assignment?" he asked.

"I never turn down work," she informed him. "But this is going to be a huge challenge." Not that she wasn't up to challenges. She would just have to pick up hints from his behavior. And hopefully from his daughters and the nanny. "It's a little like being asked to paint something beautiful on a canvas and then someone blindfolds you just before you begin."

Feeling as if she'd ignored the housekeeper long

enough, Kennon stopped talking about work and smiled at the woman who appeared to be taking in every word that had just been said. "How are you feeling, Edna?"

"A little shaky," she confessed.

"Well, this will help," Kennon promised. Since there was no table for the bowl, Kennon volunteered her services instead. "Here, I'll hold the bowl and plate up for you while you eat—unless you'd like me to feed you," she offered.

"I haven't had to be fed since I was in a high chair," Edna told her, slowly pulling herself up into a sitting position and trying to get comfortable. "I'll do this myself, thank you." With that she took the spoon from Kennon.

The woman looked exceedingly weak to her. "I'll still hold the bowl," Kennon told her cheerfully. Anticipating Edna's protest, she was quick to add, "It's no problem."

About to say something, Edna stopped and then shifted her eyes to Simon. Shaking her head, she said, "She's a stubborn one."

"I hadn't noticed," Simon replied dryly. He looked at Edna, debating whether to remain down here with the woman or not. Right now, he felt like a fifth wheel—or, technically, a third one. "You'll be all right if I leave you alone?"

Kennon cleared her throat. "In case you haven't noticed, Doctor, she's not alone. I'm here."

"I'm assuming that you'll be going home, or to your office, or wherever it is that you go to, soon," he emphasized.

"Eventually." Business was slow and if something

came up, Nathan would either handle it, or call her. Either way, she was covered.

A smile began to curve the corners of Edna's mouth. "It appears that I am in good hands, Doctor. Thank you for your concern, but I'm sure that I will be just fine."

With a nod, and not wanting to get drawn into another conversation, Simon withdrew. His intention was to go up to his room. He had no plans beyond that. His days and nights were still comprised of a myriad of tiny, disjointed pieces, glittering, winking mosaics that made up patterns with no rhyme or reason.

But his intentions were abruptly arrested as he passed the kitchen once again. The strong aroma wafting from the large pot on the stove reminded him that he hadn't eaten breakfast. Nor could he really remember if he'd had dinner the night before. He'd ordered out for the girls and Edna, but hadn't eaten with them. Or alone, either.

His stomach reminded him that it did need tribute occasionally.

He supposed there was nothing to be lost by sampling a little of what that decorator with the smart mouth had made.

Pausing, he put a little of the soup into one of the remaining bowls. It amounted to barely more than a couple of large spoonfuls. He sipped a small spoonful. It was followed by a second. And then a third. By then he decided that he should have a proper serving.

No sense in wasting her efforts, he told himself just before he set the filled bowl down on the counter and dug in.

He didn't hear her come into the kitchen, but he saw her reflection in the black oven door, which was just above the stove and at eye level. He braced himself for another assault of rhetoric.

But she didn't cross to him. Instead, she quietly withdrew from the room, leaving him in peace to eat her soup.

Maybe the woman was intuitive after all.

But he doubted it.

Chapter Five

"Is she going to be coming back, Daddy?"

Madelyn's questions came right on the heels of the quick greeting she'd given him when he picked her and her sister up from school that afternoon. She looked at him pointedly after she scrambled into the backseat and sat down beside Meghan.

"Is who coming back?" Simon asked absently as he helped Meghan fasten her seat belt and then tested it to make sure it had snapped into place.

"Kennon," Meghan piped up. She smiled broadly as she gave the absent woman her seal of approval. "I like her, Daddy."

He glanced at his younger daughter. Meghan was the warm and sunny one. She took after Nancy, while Madelyn was more like him. Cautious. At least, until today, he amended.

He laughed shortly, shaking his head. "You like everyone," he told her.

"But Kennon's nice," Madelyn insisted. Her tone said that she usually agreed with her father, but in this one instance, Meghan was actually right. "So, is she?"

"Is she what?" Simon asked, getting back into the driver's seat. He quickly strapped himself in, then started up the vehicle.

Madelyn sighed loudly. "Is she coming back?" she repeated her initial question. "Daddy, aren't you paying attention?" she asked in exasperation.

Now she sounded like her mother, the few times that Nancy had lost her patience with him. Even Madelyn's inflection was the same. He had to stop doing this, Simon silently lectured himself.

"Sorry," he apologized, easing away from the curb and waiting for his turn to enter the flow of snail-paced traffic. "My mind was wandering."

"Where did it go, Daddy?" Meghan asked. At six she was a walking mass of question marks. "I didn't see it go. Is it really little?" she asked, trying to lean forward. The seat belt restrained her and she wriggled in her seat.

"No, stupid," Madelyn said impatiently. "Daddy just means he was thinking of something else."

Which led Meghan to another question. "What, Daddy? What were you thinking of?" the little girl asked him eagerly.

Madelyn joined forces with Meghan and added her voice to her sister's. "Yeah, what, Daddy?"

He glanced over his shoulder at their inquisitive, lively little faces. God, he wished he could be that young again. That young and able to bounce back from anything.

He couldn't tell them that he was thinking about their mother, couldn't chance bringing them down because he was a stickler for the truth. So he lied. It was kinder all around that way.

"I was just thinking about what two little girls might want for dinner."

"Us, Daddy? Are the two little girls us?" Meghan asked eagerly, her green eyes shining.

"Yes," he replied. Finally out on the main thoroughfare, he glanced at Meghan in the rearview mirror. The flow of traffic picked up. "The two little girls are you and your sister."

"You still didn't answer my question, Daddy," Madelyn reminded him.

Madelyn was like a bulldog when she got hold of something, he thought. She didn't let loose until she had what she wanted. In this case, it was answers to her question. This time, he needed no prompting to recall the topic.

"You really liked this woman?"

It was Meghan who piped up first. "Oh, yes, Daddy. She smells good."

"Not an unimportant quality," he agreed, amused. The light turned yellow. Alone he would have sped through. But he had the girls with him, so he slowed down and waited. The light turned red a beat later. "Anything else?"

"She talked to us," Meghan added brightly with enthusiasm.

"All right." He had already gathered that. So far, he wasn't sure he understood what the girls' excitement about the woman was. At least, not on the junior level. Had they been teenage boys instead, he would have easily understood the attraction. Petite, she appeared to have a shapely form and her facial bone structure was such that a plastic surgeon would have wept with envy.

His powers of observation had obviously become more acute.

When had that happened?

Madelyn, his resident little wise woman, apparently had picked up on the fact that he didn't fully understand what her sister was telling him.

"No, Daddy, she talked *to* us," she emphasized. "Not *at* us, *to* us. She treats like us people. Like Edna does," she added in an effort to make him understand what she meant.

And as he didn't, Simon thought. He knew he was struggling and somewhat remiss in his job as a parent.

As their *only* parent.

This was tough going. It wasn't that he didn't love them—he did, but he just couldn't show it, didn't know how to show it or how to express it. Moreover, although they were his blood, he had trouble relating to them.

His own parents had been distant while he was growing up and thus he had no real clue how to talk to his own children, not in the way he felt that Madelyn meant.

That sort of communication had been up to his wife and Edna. They had both dealt with the day-to-day business of the girls' lives. He had never developed the knack. Work became his sanctuary, his excuse, his very validation. His contact with them heretofore was cursory. He only interacted with them on occasion, making sure that they were fed and clothed and thriving, at least physically. As for how they were faring emotionally, well, that was something else again, something he felt that he wasn't equipped to handle. But that was all right as long as they'd had their mother.

But now they didn't have her.

He knew that he had shortcomings. He'd never pretended otherwise. Serious shortcomings, highlighted by the fact that a complete stranger, practically walking in off the street, was better at interacting with his daughters than he was.

"Would you like Miss Cassidy to come back?" He asked the question to humor them. He assumed they'd say yes, but he wasn't prepared for the loud chorus of "Yes!" that assaulted his ears. For two rather small girls, they had powerful vocal chords when they were motivated.

"Is she going to be our new nanny?" Meghan asked.

Madelyn frowned, instantly thinking ahead. "Doesn't Edna like us anymore?"

He felt like Pandora several seconds after opening the legendary box. "Of course Edna likes you. She's just not feeling well and, no, Miss Cassidy isn't going to be your new nanny."

"Then what is she going to be?" Madelyn wanted to know.

More than likely, a pain in my butt.

Simon had no idea where that had come from or why he was so certain that it was true, but he was. There was something about the determined look in the woman's eyes as she had left the house that had put him on notice, telling him he was about to, willingly or otherwise, enter a heretofore undiscovered region.

He hoped he was wrong.

But the girls did like her, as apparently did Edna. The bottom line was that he did need to have the house furnished and he had no time to get involved in doing the job himself. Like most males over the age of five, he hated shopping. This was an additional, overwhelming chore he didn't want to burden Edna with. She had enough to handle, taking care of the girls. And besides, the woman was getting on in years.

"Miss Cassidy is going to decorate our house," he told them simply.

"You mean like for Christmas?" Meghan asked breathlessly.

"No, Christmas is in December. This is May," Madelyn informed her sister haughtily with a sniff. "Don't you know anything?"

Undaunted, Meghan shot back, "I know lots of stuff. Don't I, Daddy?" she asked, looking to her father for backup.

"Yes, you do. You both do," he added quickly. The one thing Nancy had managed to impress upon him was the need to treat the girls equally and to maintain neutrality whenever possible. "Miss Cassidy is going to be buying new furniture for the house."

"Can we help her buy the furniture?" Meghan asked eagerly.

"Well, I can't see why not. Sure, by all means, help her," he agreed.

This way, the woman would be way too busy dealing with the girls to try to rope him into coming along on any of her shopping trips. He viewed it as a win-win situation.

* * *

The moment she walked in the door, Nathan put down the bolts of cloth he was working with and sent a scrutinizing look her way, curiosity rising up in his large, brown eyes.

"So? How did it go?" he prodded.

Kennon felt not unlike someone who had just endured a marathon and was close to being out of breath, except that she hadn't run a marathon and she had absolutely no reason to feel that way.

Dropping her purse onto her desk, she sank down in her oversize, incredibly soft leather chair. "Strangely, very strangely."

"You're going to have to be a little clearer than that," Nathan told her. He pulled up a chair and planted himself beside her, a vacant vessel eagerly seeking to be filled.

Kennon began with the basic information. "The doctor has—"

"Wait, he's a doctor?" Nathan repeated the vocation as if it was one step removed from king.

"Yes, he's a doctor," she pressed on. "And he's got a brand-new two-story house that's completely empty, except for a couple of pieces of furniture here and there."

Nathan's appetite was completely engaged and in high gear. Though he only leaned forward, she could visualize him rubbing his hands together. "Great, depending on his tastes and what he wants, that should keep you busy for the next couple of months."

She frowned and shook her head. "That's just it, I don't know his tastes or what he wants."

Nathan didn't see the problem. "Ask," he all but commanded.

She looked at him incredulously. Did he think she was some shrinking violet, afraid to open her mouth? "I *did*."

"And?"

"And he said I should use my judgment."

Nathan looked two steps removed from dancing around her desk with glee.

"Even better," he enthused. "He gave you carte blanche," he said, savoring the term. "Carte blanche, Kennon," he repeated, unable to understand why she wasn't overjoyed the way he was. "That means that he won't be getting in the way or underfoot and you can create the house of your—his dreams."

That was just the problem. How would she be successful at that if she hadn't a clue of what the man's "dreams" were?

She knew that business had been slow and Nathan was visualizing profits, but that wasn't all there was to consider here.

"I have a feeling that Dr. Simon Sheffield is a very opinionated man and if I don't guess right about what he likes and doesn't like, this venture isn't going to turn out well at all."

Nathan looked at her knowingly, as if he expected her to make a rabbit materialize without the benefit of even a hat.

"Have a little faith, Kennon," he coaxed, his eyes locking with hers. "I do. Work a little of your magic. *Talk* to him a little, get the man to come out of his shell." He beamed at his mentor. He'd had his pick of people to apprentice with and observe. He'd picked her for a reason, not by chance. "I never knew anyone who could pick up on people's vibes the way you can. That's why you're so good."

A little stunned, Kennon wondered if she should be checking the parking structure for signs of a pod. "Why, Nathan, is that a compliment?"

One of his thin shoulders rose and fell in an absent shrug. "It could be construed that way," he allowed vaguely, then warned, "But if you tell anyone, I'll deny it."

Kennon smiled at him. Just when she thought she could read him like a book, down to his last disgruntled comment, Nathan surprised her. It kept things fresh, she mused.

"As long as I know, that's all that matters." His words replayed in her head and she paused abruptly, thinking.

Because she'd stopped talking, Nathan looked at her, his eyes narrowing as if he was trying to hone in on her thoughts.

"I can hear the wheels turning in your head," he told her. "What's going on in there?"

"Maybe a little strategy," she replied, considering her next move.

Nathan grinned from ear to ear. "That's my girl," he declared with feeling. The next moment, Kennon rose to her feet again and tucked her bag strap over her shoulder. "Where are you going?"

"Back to the battlefield," Kennon replied, tossing the words over her shoulder. "I intend to get to know the subject whether he likes it or not."

She had more in mind than just that, but this wasn't the time to fill Nathan in on her game plan. First she would see just how entrenched she needed to get into Dr. Sheffield's life.

And *that* was the Kennon Cassidy he knew and loved, Nathan thought. "You go get 'im, boss," he called after her.

Kennon didn't bother turning around. She had work to do.

I fully intend to, Nathan. I fully intend to.

Simon glared and willed the doorbell to be silent.

But it rang again.

Because the girls were within earshot, he swallowed the oath that rose to his lips. He didn't feel like putting up with anyone. Moreover, he wasn't expecting anyone. There wasn't anyone to expect, especially since they were new to the area and, other than the chief of surgery and the principal of the girls' school, neither of whom had any reason to be ringing his doorbell, he didn't actually know anyone yet.

Just then, Meghan ran by him like a shot, her focus, the front door.

"Hold it, Meghan!" he called out, exasperated as he came to life and ran after her. "I told you never to let anyone in."

Looking crestfallen, his younger daughter halted mid-dash, her mission suddenly aborted. "Sorry, Daddy. I was just trying to help."

He was on the verge of lecturing her that there was a right way and a wrong way to "help," but she seemed so sad and so earnest at the same time, he found he hadn't the heart to reprimand her. Instead, he decided to make no comment, feeling it might be better that way.

These days, he operated with a shorter fuse, much

shorter than usual, and he didn't want to risk saying anything in anger that would upset either one of his daughters. Their feelings were particularly fragile and he wasn't given to apologies. He would have no idea how to reinstate himself into their favor should he ever do anything to bruise their feelings and cause them to look upon him with either fear or a childish sort of disdain.

By the time the doorbell rang for a third time, he'd reached it. Yanking the door open he all but shouted, "Yes?" only to find Kennon Cassidy standing on his doorstep. Again.

A definite sensation of déjà vu washed over him. As did an unexpected, warm feeling he immediately banked down. He did his best to collect his temper and lower his tone. "Did you forget something?"

Now here was a man whose very voice could scare off burglars, she thought. Lucky for her she wasn't faint of heart. "Yes, that you had no actual pots and pans beyond the one I used for soup."

And what did that have to do with anything? he wondered. He glanced at the large box she held. By the way she boosted it, he figured it had to be heavy. "And what? You bought a set for us?"

"No, I'm lending you a set."

As she confirmed his suspicions, Simon took the box from her. He was right, these *were* heavy. The woman was stronger than she looked.

"These are mine," she told him, following him into the house. "You can use them until we start outfitting your kitchen."

Hearing her voice, Madelyn came hurrying into the foyer to join her sister. Both girls wiggled in ahead of him, Simon noted, in their efforts to get closer to this woman who was obviously some sort of modern-day female Pied Piper.

Either that or she'd cast some kind of hypnotic spell over his daughters. He'd never seen them take to anyone so quickly. Or so eagerly.

"You came back!" Meghan cried happily, her eyes shining.

Kennon grinned at her and tousled the girl's dark hair affectionately. "Yes, I did."

"Are you going to come in?" Madelyn asked in a sophisticated tone, though it didn't hide her feelings about Kennon's return.

Kennon looked up at the girls' father. He appeared almost stoic, standing there with the box of pots in his hands.

"I don't know. Am I, Dr. Sheffield?" she asked the man.

He feigned surprise. "You're actually asking my permission?"

Her expression said that was a given—he had no idea if she was sincere or merely putting him on. He had a feeling that his decorator got her way a lot.

"It is your house, Dr. Sheffield. You can invite anyone you want, or bar them from your property just as easily."

He supposed, all things considered, it could be that easy—if he weren't dealing with wistful, turned-up little faces.

"Lucky me." And then he stepped back, giving her some room. "Come on in. The girls have already invited you. Who am I to stand in your way?"

As if it were that easy, Kennon thought. If the good doctor didn't want her here, she'd be gone in a heartbeat and they both knew it.

Even as he invited her in, he saw her turn toward her vehicle. Now what?

"Just let me get the rest of the pots and pans out of the car," she told him.

There were more? Who did she expect Edna to be cooking for? A reserve branch of the marines?

"Can we help?" Meghan asked eagerly.

Kennon paused. "That's up to your dad, but I would love some help if he says it's all right."

How had she done that? Simon wondered. How had she lobbed the ball back onto his court and stolen his team at the same time? He wondered if that was part of her business training or if executing sleights of hand like that just came naturally to her. In either case, this was not the simple, fluffy-looking woman she appeared to be at first encounter.

"Fine."

Balancing the box she'd given him and shifting it to one side against his hip, he silently gestured for his daughters to go ahead and help the woman retrieve whatever else she'd decided to bring along to "lend" him.

For once, neither Madelyn nor Meghan needed to be told twice.

Chapter Six

The next half hour was a whirl of activity. Aided
and abetted by her two pint-size assistants, Kennon
took over the kitchen and within exactly twenty-eight
minutes produced a small pork loin that tantalized with
an aroma that whispered of Italian herbs and various
grated cheeses. There was a side dish of brown rice,
initially cooked in chicken broth, that had been mixed
with shredded asparagus, shredded carrots and shredded
zucchini, to mention only the three main vegetables that
had been added to it.

His daughters, avowed vegetable haters both, couldn't
dig in fast enough.

Simon began to think he'd opened up his house to a
sorceress. She had definitely charmed his daughters and
his housekeeper within an inch of their lives. Edna was
still in the living room, eating the same dinner that was
being served in the kitchen. Kennon had seen to that,

bringing out a full plate for the woman before finally sitting down at the table herself.

There was conversation at the table, something that had been seriously lacking in the last year. Both girls were eager to snare the sorceress's attention. For her part, the woman was equal handed, giving both the same amount of attention.

No doubt about it, she was good. And, he supposed, he could learn from her. Meghan, and especially Madelyn, looked happier than he remembered them being in a long time.

"You know, if this decorating thing doesn't work out for you..." Simon began after he realized that he had cleaned his plate not once, but twice. Only the fear of settling in for an evening nap rather than doing the work he'd brought home had kept him from taking a third helping. "...you could always get a job as a chef," he continued.

Or as an all-round whirling dervish, he added silently.

Humor highlighted her face, fluidly moving from her lips to her eyes. She looked very pleased with herself. He supposed she had every right to be.

"I'll keep that in mind." Her eyes captured his.

He had no idea what she was thinking, nor why he felt so intrigued by her.

"Could I count on a letter of recommendation from you?" She asked so straight-faced he actually thought she was serious for a moment. Until the slight telltale curve of the corners of her mouth returned and subsequently gave her away.

Simon shrugged. "Why not?" he replied.

"High praise, indeed," she quipped dryly. "Don't

worry, the only recommendation I'm interested in has to do with decorating." She had no intention of doing anything else, ever. "I've been in the decorating business for a number of years and I've ridden out a lot of highs and lows. This dip in the economy is all part of that."

Although she had to admit it would be nice to get back to the point where she was juggling assignments, looking for a way to squeeze yet another one in, rather than waiting for the phone to ring so that she had something to do. Until this assignment—if indeed it actually was one—had come along, she'd quietly begun paying Nathan out of her personal account because the business account was close to flatlining.

"And speaking of references," she threw in, switching gears back to his initial comment, "my references are available for viewing anytime you'd like to look them over." She had a website, plus an actual physical file where she kept her letters of reference, all of which were glowing.

But Simon waved away her offer, uninterested. "No need," he told her.

She looked at him in surprise. He struck her as a belt-and-suspenders kind of man, taking precautions, making sure everything was on the up-and-up—and then devising a backup plan just in case. Did this mean he'd changed his mind about hiring her for the job?

"You don't want to see my references?" she asked, wondering why he'd suddenly switched courses. Had she said something to offend him?

"Recommendations from people I don't know don't impress me," he told her. "An enthusiastic one from someone I know or have dealt with—like Ms. Sommers—does. She seemed to be very high on your ability to, in her words, turn a 'sow's ear into a silk purse.'"

Since Maizie was her aunt, the endorsement could be misconstrued as nepotism. But while Maizie would never bad-mouth anyone, she would never praise anyone if she felt their work was lacking in any way. She was far too honest to lie.

"Nothing quite that drastic," Kennon assured him. "But I have been able to turn some pretty awful rooms into lovely extensions of the client's home, bringing up the total value of the house." Warming to her subject, she rose from the table, ready to make a quick run to her vehicle. "I've got an album of my work in the car that I can show you."

His words stopped her in her tracks.

Wiping his mouth, Simon retired his fork. "You can save yourself the trouble, Miss Cassidy. I don't have time to handle the job myself and I certainly don't have time to conduct any more lengthy interviews."

Any more? Kennon bit her tongue to keep from echoing the last part of his statement incredulously. Did this qualify as a lengthy interview in his mind? On what planet? He hadn't asked her for any kind of information, any backup statements, nothing. This didn't qualify as an interview. It didn't even make the grade for a run-of-the-mill conversation.

Don't antagonize the gift horse, Kennon, she cautioned herself.

Putting on her brightest smile, she asked, "So then I'm hired?"

Simon raised his deep blue eyes to hers, silently asking what part of his statement she didn't understand. Of course she was hired—unless she had a comprehension problem.

"That's what I just said."

Not really. Her smile never shifted.

The man needed to work on his communication skills. She wondered if he was just as obscure and distant with his patients when he spoke to them. Heart patients, she would think, would want to have their hands held, would want to be comforted and put at their ease. They would want to know that their surgeon *cared*. There was absolutely nothing about this exceedingly handsome, exceedingly sexy, reserved man that came close to even hinting that he cared about the people he operated on. Was it a protective device? A mechanism he employed so that he *couldn't* get close to anyone, just in case they didn't make it?

Focus on what's important. You've got bills to pay, Kennon. "Thank you," she told him. "I can start tomorrow. Tonight if you like."

He shook his head. Her eagerness made him feel tired. It was almost as if her energy was growing only because it was sapping his.

"What I'd like," he informed her, "is to go to my study and get back to the paper I was working on yesterday. The paper with the quickly approaching deadline."

She backed away quickly. It did no good to get a client stirred up about anything except color schemes. "Of course. So when can I speak with you?" she asked so she could plan accordingly.

"You just did," he pointed out, rising from the table. "This was very good," he told her, as if he was measuring out each word carefully, taking them out of some invisible bank account and leaving a deficit in their wake.

Kennon watched him leave the room, heading for the stairs. She did her best not to let her frustration show in her face. No matter what he thought, she was really going to need to speak to him about the house. Decorating was a matter of personal taste—in this case, his. She wasn't about to impose her own aesthetics on him. Aside from perhaps a fondness for blue, she had a feeling that their individual preferences would most likely clash fiercely.

"He doesn't mean anything by it, Miss. He's just hurting."

Edna's voice floated in from the living room, cutting into her thoughts. Giving the girls a quick, fleeting smile, Kennon cocked her head and looked around the side into the living room.

Edna was sitting up on the sofa, propped up exactly where she and the girls had left her. The plate Kennon had brought out to her earlier lay on top of the black-lacquered folding TV tray, which she'd brought with her expressly for Edna's usage until the nanny was literally back on her feet.

After first encouraging the girls to have another serving, she left them to finish their dinner and crossed over to the living room and Edna.

"I understand," Kennon said, lowering her voice so that it wouldn't carry. "But I need to know what Dr. Sheffield wants me to do with the house besides just 'fill' it."

The girls had heard her anyway. "I've got pictures," Meghan volunteered happily.

Kennon's attention instantly shifted. Something was

far better than nothing. "You mean pictures of your old house?"

Ignoring her older sister's pointed scowl, Meghan nodded. "Daddy said to pack away our pictures, but I wanted them with me so I could look at them. Mama gave me the album. I didn't want to throw it away or lose it," she explained.

Gutsy little thing, Kennon thought with admiration. Simon Sheffield seemed as if he was capable of casting a large shadow over his children. Secretly defying the man took courage.

"Daddy didn't want you to throw it away, stupid," Madelyn chided. "He just wanted to put everything we wanted to keep into that big storage place." Seeing that her sister still didn't grasp the concept of what she was saying, Madelyn explained what storage was. "It's a big room for all our stuff, but it's not in the house."

Meghan didn't look as if she believed what she was being told. "Then where is it?"

"Someplace else," Madelyn told her, this time letting her shortened fuse show.

Pictures would definitely help, Kennon thought. But she wasn't sure just how much they'd help until she had a basic question answered. Did the surgeon want to get away from everything that reminded him of the life he'd lost, or would he want to recapture that feeling? Or would it be a blending of old and new?

She definitely needed help in coming to the right conclusion.

"Why don't you two carry your plates to the sink?" she suggested.

The two were instantly on their feet, grabbing up their plates as well as the silverware they'd used. Both acted as if bussing a table was a treat rather than a chore. Kennon couldn't help wondering if the doctor knew how lucky he was.

She turned toward Edna. She'd given the girls the chore so that she could talk to the nanny privately. The questions in her head were multiplying. "You said that Dr. Sheffield was still hurting. Over his wife's death?" Kennon guessed.

"Yes."

She could see by the look in the older woman's eyes that this was not an easy subject for her either. The doctor's wife must have been a very special person to merit such fierce love and loyalty.

"He blames himself," Edna told her simply.

"Why?" Kennon could think of only one reason. "Was he to blame?"

"No!" Edna cried with feeling. "It's because she took his place."

"His place?" Kennon echoed. She tried to make sense of the answer. "You mean like on a plane?"

Taking a deep breath, Edna started at the beginning. "Dr. Sheffield belongs to Doctors Without Borders. He joined because Dr. Nancy wanted him to. He was supposed to go to Somalia but at the last moment, his last triple-bypass patient took a turn for the worse a few hours after the surgery. The doctor didn't want to leave the man in someone else's hands, so Dr. Patterson—that was Mrs. Sheffield's professional name—told him not to worry. She said she'd go in his place."

"Dr. Sheffield's wife was a cardiovascular surgeon, too?" Kennon asked incredulously.

Edna smiled with pride, tears shimmering in her eyes. "My Nancy was a general surgeon. In a pinch, she could perform almost any kind of regular surgery that needed doing." Edna's voice grew very quiet as she added, "When the tsunami hit, she was one of the ones who was swept away."

"Oh. I'm so sorry to hear that," Kennon told her, genuinely feeling the woman's pain. But Edna had caught her attention with what she'd said before recounting the abilities of the doctor's late wife. "Excuse me, you said 'your Nancy…'" Kennon's voice trailed off as she waited for a clarification. The girls' nanny couldn't mean that the surgeon's wife was her daughter. Could she? Dr. Sheffield wouldn't be treating his former mother-in-law like one of the servants, would he?

The tears that shone in Edna's eyes threatened to come spilling out. She blinked them back with effort, but a few fell, sliding down her cheek.

"I raised that girl from the time she was an infant. Both her parents were busy earning a living—much the way Dr. Sheffield and Dr. Patterson were," she added. "Because we had such a close relationship, when her own two little ones came along, she asked me to take care of them." She did her best to collect herself. "I was thrilled to be of use to her. I love those girls as if they were my own."

Kennon didn't doubt it. "I take it that by moving from San Francisco to Southern California, Dr. Sheffield felt that he needed a fresh start?"

Edna nodded her head. "He never said so in so many words, but that's what I think, yes."

Kennon was already processing what she'd been told. "Then what we'll probably need is only the slightest touch of the past, with the main emphasis being on the future." Having voiced her thoughts out loud, she looked at Edna to see if the older woman agreed with her.

The nanny took another deep breath, as if to push herself forward.

"I think that would be for the best. Miss Nancy would have wanted Dr. Sheffield to move on. She wouldn't have wanted him to be this unhappy. She was always teasing him about being too serious," she said fondly, remembering. And then she looked up at Kennon, as if appealing for her help. "This is way beyond that, and he needs to laugh again."

Again. So the man was capable of actually laughing, Kennon thought. That was good to know. It meant that there was something for her to work with.

"Well, I don't know if I can make him laugh, but we'll really try to get him to smile again," she promised Edna.

At that moment, Madelyn burst back into the room and headed straight toward them. Madelyn looked at Kennon pointedly. "Anything else?" the little girl asked.

Right on her sister's heels, not to be outdone, Meghan echoed in a louder voice, "Yeah, anything else?"

For tonight, Kennon thought, she just wanted to immerse herself in the interactions of the family. Since the good doctor wasn't down here with them, the girls—and memories of their mother—would just have to do.

Immersing meant blending in.

"Now I'm going to go and wash the dishes," Kennon informed the girls as she got up off the arm of the sofa where she'd perched while talking to Edna.

"You wash dishes? By yourself?" Madelyn questioned, looking at up her uncertainly. "We've got a dish-washer that does that."

"Don't you have a dishwasher?" Meghan asked her, pity in her young voice.

Kennon laughed and put her arm around the younger girl's shoulders, pulling her in for a quick hug. "Yes, I do, but I never like to have things pile up in the sink so I wash them before there're too many. Besides, running the dishwasher for one person just seems sort of wasteful to me. Don't you agree?" she asked Meghan.

Thrilled to be asked for her opinion, Meghan nodded her head vigorously. Kennon had a feeling that the little girl would have easily agreed to anything that she suggested.

"You really have a way with them," Edna told her with genuine sincerity. She looked from one little girl to the other. There was approval in her voice as she said, "You seem to bring out the best in them. Do you have any children of your own?" the older woman asked, curious about this new person in their lives.

Kennon shook her head. "No."

Not that she wouldn't have wanted to have children. Several children. But before there were children, there had to be someone who could be a good husband, a good father. And if he could actually make her heart skip a beat or two, well, so much the better. If she was going to dream, she might as well go all the way.

"I never met the right man," she told Edna. And with that, she closed the subject.

"Were you the oldest in your family, then?" Edna asked. "The one your mother depended on to look out for the others?"

There were no others. Her parents were divorced

before she could get any siblings. She had always regretted that. A lot of her time as a child had been spent imagining what having a brother or sister would have been like. Even inventing an imaginary one when she was very young.

"Sorry to disappoint you, Edna," she said with a smile, "but I'm an only child."

"Then it's a true gift you have," Edna pronounced. "You've been blessed."

She didn't know about being "blessed"—it was just something that came rather naturally to her. Maybe it was even born out of that desire for a sibling. But before she could say anything to the contrary, Madelyn had caught her by one hand while, not to be left out, Meghan took hold of the other.

"Then we'll help you do the dishes," Madelyn declared.

Amused, Edna laughed. "Like I said, Miss Cassidy, you've got a gift. You're not all that bad at healing, either."

Kennon looked at her quizzically over her shoulder as she was about to be pulled away.

"I'm feeling much better, thanks to you and your chicken soup," Edna told her.

"If that's the case, that would be more due to the chicken than to me," Kennon told her. She wasn't one to take praise unless she believed she really deserved it. All she'd done in this case was try to make the woman feel a little better—and comfort food had always accomplished that for her.

The next moment, Kennon found herself being taken off to the kitchen again by her pint-size helpers. It was time to address the dishes in the sink.

"And modest, too," Edna said to herself with an approving nod. "I think you'd like her, Nancy," she said softly under her breath.

When Simon came down from his study an hour later, he expected to find the kitchen in darkness and his daughters either in their room for the night or in the family room, taking advantage of the fact that he wasn't around. He was rather strict about the amount of time they could spend watching television.

He was rather strict about most things when it came to his children.

Instead, he found the kitchen ablaze with light. Not only that, but he heard the sound of laughter coming from there, as well.

Curious, he went to the source. And discovered that the woman he'd just hired as his decorator was there, sitting at the head of the table, with his daughters flanking her on either side.

Schoolbooks were spread out on the surface of the table and, from what he could discern as he drew closer, the girls were doing homework—with a little help from the overly effervescent blonde.

Laughter, he realized as he listened and allowed it to warm him, was a sound that had been missing from their lives for much too long.

He'd been right in his earlier assessment. Apparently he'd not only hired a decorator but a sorceress, as well.

Chapter Seven

Out of the corner of her eye, Kennon saw Simon walking into the kitchen.

Even if she hadn't, she could tell he'd entered the room because of the way Madelyn and Meghan reacted. They became a little more subdued, a tiny bit less relaxed. A little more anxious to please. It was obvious to her that they loved their father, but were hemmed in by not quite knowing how to behave around him. As for the good doctor, he wasn't exactly cold—she could sense that he did care about his daughters—but he was reserved, as if he was following some sort of a strict code that only he was aware of.

Meghan saw him first. "Daddy, Kennon's teaching me to write," she declared proudly.

Simon was paying a none-too-shabby tuition so that Meghan and Madelyn would receive the best parochial education possible. Even so, he'd been debating getting a tutor for the younger one because Meghan was having a harder time learning than her sister ever had. Apparently all he'd had to do to insure her improvement was get his house decorated.

He looked at the woman who had burst into his life like an unforecast hurricane. "Master chef, gifted teacher, instant nanny and, oh, yes, a top-flight decorator." There was a touch of sarcasm in his voice as he ticked off the talents she'd displayed today. "Anything you can't do, Miss Cassidy?"

Yes, fathom why I seem to annoy you so much, Kennon thought. She wasn't about to say this out loud and merely rose to her feet. "I'll let you know if and when it comes up." Aware that she had stayed far longer than she'd intended, and most likely in the doctor's opinion had more than overstayed her welcome, Kennon looked at her self-appointed assistants and said, "I've got to be going now."

The girls both looked disappointed that she was leaving. "Oh, do you have to?" Meghan pouted. "I want to write some more."

"Practice for me," Kennon encouraged. "And yes, I really do have to go now. But I'll be back tomorrow," she promised the sisters. When she saw the uncertain look in their eyes, she sensed that they'd had promises made that had been broken. It wasn't much of a leap for her to guess who had broken them. She tried to reassure the girls. "We have work to do, remember?"

Clearly surprised at how quickly his daughters had taken to this almost total stranger, Simon asked, "What kind of work?"

Kennon gathered her things together and deposited them in her purse. She snapped the lock. "The girls and I are going to look over a few catalogues I'm bringing over for them so we can get some ideas on how to decorate their rooms."

He hadn't planned on seeing the woman again so soon. They hadn't even worked out the terms of her fee yet. Not that money was a problem. That was definitely at the bottom of his list of concerns. "I suppose I'll have to pay you extra for that."

"Maybe I should pay you," she countered. When he looked at her quizzically, she said by way of an explanation, "Your daughters are charming, Dr. Sheffield, and a lot of fun to be around."

And I have an idea that you would be, too, if you gave yourself half a chance.

She raised her voice so that it would carry to the living room. "Good night, Edna. I'm glad you're feeling better." Turning to her younger pupil, she said, "Remember, Meghan, practice your *F*'s. They need just a tiny little bit of work before they're perfect."

Meghan clearly lapped up the praise. The spark in her eyes showed a determination to follow the instructions to the letter. "Yes, ma'am," she agreed cheerfully.

"See you tomorrow, Madelyn," Kennon said warmly. "Good night, Doctor," she murmured with a nod toward him, then, picking up her purse, she headed toward the front door.

For a moment, Simon stared after her, feeling a little disoriented and bemused, like someone who had survived a sudden, unexpected attack of unseasonable weather. He supposed, in the final analysis, it was a lucky thing that the woman had just happened by here this morning instead of, say, next week. It had made things a lot easier for him.

He thought of Edna. It was doubtful that the nanny would be completely well by morning. And he would have to get down to the hospital early. Tomorrow was the day he would meet with the other members of the Newport Cardiovascular Group.

He needed someone to take care of Madelyn and Meghan. Again.

Coming to life, Simon hurried after Kennon. "Miss Cassidy—"

Surprised to hear him calling her, Kennon turned at the front door and looked behind her. The doctor crossed to her with some alacrity. She waited until he was almost next to her, then said, "It's Kennon."

Why was she telling him that? "I know your first name."

All this formality on his part definitely made her feel uncomfortable. "And if I'm going to be working here for you, I'd like you to use it."

"'If?'" he questioned. Was she having second thoughts? Was this going to turn into a ploy for more money after all?

"Figure of speech," Kennon conceded. "I think I can do your house justice, Dr. Sheffield."

The different ways a house could be decorated was not even remotely high on his list of priorities. His main requirement was that it didn't stir up any memories for him—and that it didn't wind up being too cluttered.

"Yes, I'm sure you'll do a fine job." He was about to let it go at that, then decided to give her the only rule he wanted her to adhere to. "As long as the decor isn't Early American."

Finally, she thought triumphantly, an opinion. "You don't like Early American?"

Actually, he didn't. But because his late wife had favored Early American, everything in their house had been decorated in that style. There were four-poster canopied beds both in the master bedroom and the girls' bedroom, and distressed tables served as accents in the various rooms. The kitchen table and chairs looked as if they could have come straight out of George Washington's home. So had everything else in the house. He had wanted something more modern, but had kept his peace.

"No, I don't," Simon said, answering her question truthfully. He wondered if Edna had mentioned their decor in San Francisco to Kennon. He had no desire to get into any sort of discussion as to why his previous house had been decorated in Early American. Granted, Kennon Cassidy had probably the most sympathetic blue eyes he'd ever seen, but he didn't want her sympathy, or anyone else's for that matter.

"Good to know," she said, looking as if she meant it. "We'll definitely go another path," Kennon promised. And then she flashed a pleased smile at him. "See? That wasn't so hard, was it, Doctor?"

"What wasn't so hard?" he asked, unclear as to what she meant.

"Telling me what you like—or in this case, what you don't like. That's all I need," she reiterated. "Just a few well-placed words. Hints, if you will. I'll bring you photographs tomorrow."

He was about to tell her that he had no interest in seeing any photographs, that as long as the furniture was functional and above all, new, that was all he required. But if it made her happy to think she had to show him photographs, so be it. There was a far more important detail to discuss.

In the background, Edna sneezed three times in succession, as if to underscore what he was about to ask and the urgency with which it needed to be regarded. "How early can you be here tomorrow?"

Kennon had no difficulty in putting two and two together quickly. Okay, so he didn't want her for her decorating talent—something he actually hadn't seen for himself yet—he wanted her for her other attributes. She could live with that. It was something to build on. Every relationship she had with a client was different and unique, and this definitely went straight to the head of the line.

Instead of giving Simon a direct answer, her reply told him that she understood his dilemma and would take care of it. "I can take the girls to school again for you if you like."

Simon didn't like being second-guessed, especially not so accurately. But since Kennon Cassidy was making herself available to him in ways that went above and beyond her job description, he decided it was a small price to pay in exchange for bailing him out.

"Good," he said. "Thank you."

Just then, she caught her new client looking at her the way a man didn't look at his decorator. As if she was affecting things that were far from cerebral. Something inside of her responded and suddenly felt extremely warm.

She recognized the sensation. She'd had it before. She didn't want it again.

She needed, Kennon thought, to take precautions so that it *didn't* happen again.

"Don't mention it," she murmured. "I'll see you tomorrow at eight." With that, Kennon turned abruptly away before this warm feeing inside her could multiply and spread—like any typical disease.

"Right. Thanks," he called after her even as he wondered if he was taking the first step in a direction he shouldn't be going. A direction he might very well live to regret eventually.

He couldn't put his finger on it. He wasn't the kind of man who put any faith in so-called gut feelings because, to his recollection, he'd never experienced any that had actually panned out.

But an unsettled feeling undulated through him right now as he watched the woman walking away. It gave him more than a little pause.

He'd actually *noticed* her. Not as an entity, not as just another human being sharing a given space on this planet with him, but as a woman. An exceedingly compelling, enthusiastic, beautiful woman.

He wasn't comfortable with that.

Wasn't happy that traits such as attractiveness or sensuality, both of which she seemed to have in spades, were slowly, insidiously, seeping into his world, making themselves known. Bringing colors into his current black-and-white life.

As he did with most things that disturbed him, Simon shut the thoughts away and went back to working, this time on his paper.

In the morning, he might be able to see things differently, placing them in their proper perspective.

It was something to hope for, even if he didn't really place any stock in hope.

* * *

Almost a week had gone by.

Five whole days and she was no closer to understanding the enigma that was Dr. Simon Sheffield than she'd been that first morning when she'd rung his doorbell.

Granted, they had gotten around to working out the terms of the fee for her services, but those services involved decorating, not ferrying the girls to and from school or sticking around to help them with their homework or whipping up dinner for them and Edna.

Not that she would have charged him for that, but they hadn't gotten around to her doing *anything* that he would be paying her for. That had to change.

She made up her mind to talk to the reclusive surgeon when he came home that evening. With that in mind, she gathered the girls to her and got to work. There was a dinner to make—and a cheering section to employ.

"You know, if I'd wanted to be a housekeeper, I would have applied for that job," Kennon told Simon the moment he walked in and shut the front door behind him.

Taking her literally, Simon said, "There wasn't anything to apply for. I wasn't looking for a housekeeper." Guessing that this might be about money and her concern that she hadn't done anything "professional" to earn it, he took out his checkbook. "How much do I owe you?"

This was coming out of left field. "For what?" she asked, mystified.

"For your time," he said, feeling as if he was stating the obvious.

"I charge by the hour," she informed him. They'd

been all through this earlier this week. "*When* I'm decorating, not when I'm grating cheese."

What did grating cheese have to do with it? "Come again?"

She smiled. Kennon had a feeling that he liked to focus on one thing at a time. "Dinner is chicken parmesan," she told him.

The patient list he'd acquired from the retiring partner in the medical firm had proven to be heavy. He'd skipped lunch to catch up on extraneous work, organizing things *his* way. The mention of food had his stomach all but sitting up and begging. He nodded, tempted to ask how soon before dinner would be on the table.

"Sounds good."

Back to the point, she thought. A point she obviously was going to have to hit him over the head with. "Doctor, I'd like to begin working on your house."

"Then go ahead," he told her with a wave of his hand. Since she was making no reference to the check, he slipped his checkbook back into his pocket. "I've already told you that you have the job."

"And you really won't accompany me to any of the furniture stores?" Rather than answer, he gave her a look that told her what he thought of spending time shopping for *anything,* much less furniture. "Not even one store?" she pressed, holding up a single finger in front of him.

Her index finger was so close to his face that he reacted instinctively, wrapping his hand around it to move the digit away. He'd intended to push her finger down. Instead, something strange, fast and hot seemed to zip through him, not unlike an electric current, the moment his hand touched hers.

A beat later, he recovered himself, pushed her hand

down and shook his head. "I don't have the time," he informed her.

Kennon looked over her shoulder and fell back on her secret weapon. She cleared her throat, and suddenly Madelyn and Meghan came running into the room to greet him.

Meghan, the live wire of the duo, grabbed her father's hand, tugged on it and immediately begged, "Please, Daddy, come with us."

"Come with you where?" he asked, confused.

He loved them both—how could he not? But he had never been a demonstrative kind of man, nor was he really very vocal. With nothing to fall back on as an example and no one to defer to, Simon hadn't a clue how to really relate to either one of his daughters. They were little people, visitors from a world he was completely unfamiliar with. His own childhood seemed as if it had happened eons ago and nothing stood out—nothing could be singled out as an occurrence to remember forever.

"To the furniture store," Madelyn told him, picking up the thread from her sister. "Kennon's taking us with her tomorrow to see what we like."

"I've decided to start with their rooms first," Kennon explained, since the girls at least were eager to give their input.

"Come with us, Daddy," Meghan begged. "We want you there."

"Yes, please, Daddy," Madelyn chimed in. And then came the crowning touch. Guilt. "We never do anything with you."

He raised his eyes to Kennon's face. This seemed a bit too organized to him.

"This your idea?" he asked.

It was a rhetorical question. Why else would his daughters suddenly begin pleading for him to go with them to a furniture store, of all places? They'd never behaved like this before.

"What?" Kennon asked innocently. "That the girls want to spend some time with their father?" She mentally crossed her fingers behind her back. "No, they came up with that all by themselves."

"Most kids ask for trips to amusement parks, not furniture stores," he pointed out.

"What can I say? Your girls are exceptionally mature for their ages." And then she dropped the teasing tone. "Besides, I suspect that it's a matter of taking what they can get." When he looked at her, a question entering his dark eyes, she elaborated. "Amusement parks are all-day commitments. A furniture store is an hour and a half, tops. Maybe they're trying to break you in slowly."

Simon was surprised when she moved in closer to him.

Kennon glanced over to the girls and said, "Excuse us for a minute, girls." Taking hold of Simon's arm, she guided him over to one side of the room. She knew she was crossing a line and that he probably wouldn't appreciate her doing so, but he had to be made to understand before it was too late.

"I think it's pretty clear that your daughters want you in their lives, Doctor. I'd say that makes you pretty lucky and I'd suggest that you take them up on it." She saw a flicker of annoyance entering his eyes. This would be where most people would back off. But most people didn't have her ability to empathize with children. She plowed on. "It won't be long before they'll just be streaks across a room as they dash out the door to go off with their friends. After that'll come boys and college, and all this will be just a memory. A memory you won't have," she emphasized, "if you don't do anything with them now."

He was a private man and he didn't like anyone meddling in his life. But he supposed the woman did have a point, and she knew it, too.

"You're going to keep talking until I give in, aren't you?"

Her mouth curved just enough to tell him that he was right. "Just thinking of you—and them," Kennon added deliberately.

Right, he thought sarcastically. And while she was *thinking,* she wasn't above manipulating the situation *and* the players to get what she wanted. Him at the furniture store. Still, he was forced to admit that he hadn't been as available to the girls as he should have been. But that was, for the most part, because he didn't know what to say.

"Tomorrow's Saturday," Kennon was telling him. "You do have the time to spare."

How did she know that? He frowned. "Now you're psychic?"

"No," she said simply. "Just resourceful."

Edna had been the one to tell her that Simon had become part of the Newport Beach Cardiovascular Group, which was housed in a very modern-looking two-story building located two blocks away from Blair Memorial Hospital. It took nothing for her to call the office and ask if Dr. Sheffield was going to be on call this Saturday. The woman scheduling appointments at the front desk had informed her that Dr. Champion was on call the entire weekend. It was all Kennon needed to know.

"Resourceful," Simon repeated, scrutinizing the dynamo before him. "I'd ask you what that meant, but I have a feeling I'm better off not knowing."

Simon sighed inwardly. Though he wouldn't admit it out loud, the woman had made a valid point. And there was the fact that he had made a silent vow to Nancy at her funeral to become more actively involved in their daughters' lives. So far, he'd only managed to live up to his word in the most marginal sense. He supposed that spending a few hours with them on Saturday, even if it was in the pursuit of furnishing their bedrooms, would be a decent start.

He capitulated.

"What time?" he asked Kennon.

She had anticipated at least another round of going back and forth, if not more, before she wore him down. This was almost too easy. Maybe he *was* a reasonable man after all.

"Then you'll come?" she asked, relieved that she could stop playing at being his conscience.

Damn, but the woman had one hell of a radiant smile, he thought. It was one of those rare smiles that seemed to instantly pull you in and made you feel that all was right with the world.

He caught himself looking at her left hand, wondering why there wasn't a wedding band, or at least an engagement ring, on her finger. For the first time since she had steamrolled into his life, he found himself wondering about her backstory.

As if to deny the very thought, Simon replied in a

voice devoid of all emotion, "That would be the natural supposition for my asking you about the time."

Kennon was tempted to tell him that he needed to loosen up a little, for the girls' sake as well as his own, but for now this was enough progress for one day. One step at a time, that was all she could logically hope for. Every journey began with a single step and ended with another one many, many steps later.

Dr. Sexy Mouth had just taken his first, Kennon thought with satisfaction. Now the trick was to keep him going until he reached the destination where he needed to be.

"Girls," she called out, turning around to face them again. "Your dad's going to be coming with us tomorrow."

He wasn't prepared for the enthusiastic squeals and cheers, nor did he expect to have two overjoyed little girls rush up and, for all intents and purposes, effectively "surround" him.

No, he wasn't prepared for it, but he had to admit he rather liked it. Liked, too, the wide, satisfied smile he saw on his decorator's face. A man could easily get lost in that face.

The next moment, he turned away from Kennon and focused only on Madelyn and Meghan. It was a lot less unsettling that way.

Chapter Eight

How one trip multiplied into two and a single, one-time-only exclusive Saturday outing mysteriously led to another—and another—in the two Saturdays that followed was something that Simon felt he needed to examine at length when he had the time. All he knew was that it'd happened so effortlessly, so naturally, that, at the time, he wasn't even aware of it. Wasn't aware of saying yes to Kennon until after the fact.

Thinking back to how all this *shopping* came about was a little like searching for the seam in a skirt that appears to be seamless. You knew it wasn't possible, there had to be a seam *somewhere,* but at first—and second—glance, it certainly looked to be without a beginning or an end.

In other words, it seemed to be continuous.

He also knew he had to put a stop to it before it became a Saturday-morning ritual to wander through furniture stores and import shops with his daughters on either side of him and the ever-effervescent interior decorator leading the way.

Simon decided to make his stand on the fourth Saturday morning. Like clockwork, Madelyn and Meghan came into his room, rushing now instead of approaching hesitantly as they had that first Saturday when he had supposedly agreed to go to just *one* store and only to purchase bedroom furniture for them. Emboldened by their previous successes and by the headway they had made edging into their father's world, this morning Madelyn and Meghan were energetic instead of the reserved girls they had been, and now burst into his bedroom with no qualms.

Bouncing onto the bed, Meghan narrowly missed landing on his chest. Completely oblivious to the near collision, she scrambled up closer to him. "Guess what, Daddy?" she cried, her voice only a couple of decibels lower than a shout.

"You're both getting married and moving out by noon," he murmured, doing his best to come to.

Meghan giggled. "You're funny, Daddy."

Yes, he was, he realized, a little surprised himself. Somewhere along the line amid these safaris to out-of-the-way shops that were so far off the beaten path there *was* no path in sight, he had somehow developed a sense of humor.

Or something very closely resembling one.

Simon wasn't exactly certain how that had come about. But he suspected, if he examined its origins, it had something to do with self-defense, as well as the woman who kept appearing on his doorstep six mornings a week with the same regularity as the sunrise.

"You're not guessing," Madelyn pointed out, climbing onto the bed beside her sister.

At this hour of the morning, his brain moved with the speed of an arthritic gazelle. He let out a long breath.

"Okay, I give up. What?" he asked, looking at Meghan and then Madelyn.

"Today Kennon said we're going shopping for *your* stuff," Meghan told him proudly, beating out her sister, who clearly wanted to be the one to tell him. But Meghan had always been the one who could talk faster.

Maybe his brain was still a little foggy, but how was that any different from the other excruciating Saturday-morning excursions? This was all his "stuff," Simon thought. After all, he was the one who paid the bills, although he had to admit that the ones he'd seen so far amounted to a great deal less than he had initially anticipated.

Of course, he had only hearsay to go on. From what he'd heard from other surgeons whose wives had gone on decorating sprees, the price tags that went with renovating a room were high enough to give a man a nosebleed. Kennon, apparently, was a "bargain" shopper who succeeded in uncovering bargains that didn't look as if they came from a discount house.

"My stuff," he repeated, watching Meghan and waiting for more explanation.

"Your bedroom stuff," Madelyn told him, casting a disgusted eye at her sister. "It was supposed to be a surprise."

"It'll be a surprise, all right," he said. "A surprise for Miss Cassidy because I'm not getting any." He gestured toward the rented bureau and the bed that had come from Castle Leasing. The store's rather trite motto was good enough for him: *Rent your castle's furnishings by the month*.

"Girls, let your father get up and get dressed," Edna admonished. She stood in the doctor's doorway, waiting for the girls to vacate the room. "Doctor Sheffield needs to eat his breakfast before he can go shopping anywhere with you."

Simon groaned. Obviously the girls' nanny had been indoctrinated by the Cassidy woman, as well. "Not you, too, Edna."

"Not me too what, Doctor?" Edna asked, looking at him with a puzzled expression on her face. Before the second round of vague verbal sparring could get under way, the doorbell rang. "Must be Miss Cassidy." Edna brightened, as did the girls. "Incredibly punctual, that one," she commented, withdrawing.

Yeah, he thought. *Even if you don't want her to be*.

"C'mon along, girls." Edna put a hand on each of their slim shoulders, guiding them out. "Leave your father in peace to get up and get dressed."

Simon seriously thought of ignoring everyone and just rolling over in bed. But he knew better. If he tried to go back to sleep, Meghan and Madelyn would make a return appearance, bouncing on his bed and tugging him out. For all he knew, that Cassidy woman might even join them. When had they stopped regarding him with quiet respect? He missed the old days, he thought grumpily.

With a sigh, Simon sat up, threw off his covers and got out of bed. Feeling somewhat groggy, he made his way into the bathroom. After he showered and woke up, he promised himself, he would tell the Cassidy woman that his days of being dragged around to various stores were definitely over.

* * *

But when he emerged twenty minutes later, showered, shaved and wearing a pair of dress slacks that were only a tad less formal than what he normally wore to the hospital, Simon never got a chance to mount his protest or attempt even so much as a minor defense.

The moment he walked into the kitchen and his interior decorator saw him, she turned on her brilliant smile—a smile that just seemed to increase in wattage every time he saw her—and started talking.

The woman's mouth should be registered with the police department as a lethal weapon. Against it he never stood a snowball's chance in hell. No one did.

She mowed him down with her rapid-fire delivery. "I thought we'd get an earlier start this morning—just as soon as you've had breakfast."

Before she could say anything else, he got his word in edgewise. "Why earlier?"

Simon sat down at the bar where Edna had placed his breakfast. Why she'd set it there rather than on the table where he usually ate was something he didn't have a chance to ponder. It was only later that he caught on to the woman's strategy. A counter and a stool created a feeling of brevity, of being in a hurry, like stopping at a diner where you went for a quick cup of coffee on your way to somewhere else.

"Because Fine Furnishings for Less is a very popular place and it fills up rather early. Name brands, low prices, large selection, it's got all the good things going for it," she told him. He noticed that she had the girls hanging on her every word, lapping them up as if she was uttering some sort of sacred truth.

"It's supposedly a secret place," she continued, "but

everyone and his brother seems to have caught on to it. I know how much you hate crowds, so if we want to avoid running into one, we need to get there early."

He could think of another way to avoid crowds. By not going to begin with. But before he stated the obvious, he had another question to ask her. If he didn't, it would drive him crazy all day.

"How do you know I hate crowds?"

He knew he'd never said as much, even though he actually did dislike finding himself surrounded by people, all but herded around like one of the cattle. It was beyond him why people enjoyed packing themselves in so tightly, pressed against their fellow man or woman in Times Square just to watch a gaudy ball fall for a total of sixty seconds. The only way anyone would ever get him there would be postmortem.

Kennon didn't answer immediately. Instead, she looked at him and the expression in her eyes said everything, as well as expressing amusement that he even asked anything so basic.

She could see he was still waiting for her to volunteer her answer. "You get, let's just say, 'quieter,' in direct proportion to the number of people in the immediate vicinity," she finally told him.

Okay, he had another weapon in his arsenal. "You know, my room is fine just the way it is."

That was a matter of opinion. Early Unmatchable was not a style and it definitely didn't go with what she was slowly doing with the rest of the house.

"It's the last holdout," she told him. "The other bedrooms have all been remodeled and decorated."

She'd had a general contractor she dealt with from time to time do a little basic rewiring and touch-up painting to complement the decor she'd chosen. Meghan, who had trouble sleeping alone at night, now shared her slumber with her favorite storybook cartoon characters, who smiled down at her from the walls. Madelyn's bedroom was all frills and femininity. Even the guest room was completely redecorated in warm yellows with a touch of light grays, suitable for male or female visitors.

And Edna's bedroom was reminiscent of her Irish roots, right down to her eyelet bedspread and warm, light green colors.

Simon's room was the last holdout, a bastion of chaos meeting style-challenged. She intended to change that.

"The object was to furnish the rooms," he reminded her. "My bedroom's furnished."

"With *rented* furniture." She said the word as if it was synonymous with pestilence and plagues. "In a year you will have paid far more than the furniture is worth." He'd probably done that in the first month, she thought. "Far more than if you'd bought your own. There's no point in throwing money away, Doctor."

His eyes met hers. Were those golden flecks he saw amid the green? "So now you're my financial planner?" he asked her. The question sounded more amused than annoyed.

That wasn't her intention—she was just trying to appeal to his sense of frugality. Anything to get him to send the furniture back where it came from.

"I wear a lot of hats in this job," she told him glibly.

"No, you don't," Meghan piped up. "You don't wear hats at all." And then she scrunched up her face as she tried to unravel the puzzle. "Are they in your trunk?" Excitement entered her eyes as she asked, "Can I see them?"

"That's another figure of speech," Madelyn said knowingly, her eyes shifting toward the woman she clearly viewed with a serious case of hero worship. Raising her eyebrows, Madelyn looked at Kennon with a silent question, her rosebud lips forming the word *right?*

Nodding, Kennon slipped her arm around each girl as she positioned herself between the two counter stools they were perched on. Counter stools that had taken a lot of negotiating on her part to get the girls to agree on. Each girl, it turned out, had her own sense of style.

As for Simon, he had said yes to every one she had pointed to, displaying absolutely no preference, the exact opposite of his daughters. He'd just wanted the experience to be over.

For whatever reason, he seemed determined to make things difficult for her, she'd thought, because without preferences—other than *not* wanting anything to be Early American—he'd given her nothing to work with. Nothing was just as bad in its own way as everything.

She was just as determined to make this entire house work. Late last night, she'd decided that the style she was going for was eclectic, something different for each room. But each room still would be in harmony with itself and, in a different way, with the others.

"I have a feeling that you're going to like this place," she told him. She saw Edna smiling to herself in the background. As usual, the nanny was on her side in this.

"What I'd really like is to have my Saturdays back," Simon responded.

Briefly, he debated volunteering to be on call next weekend just to get out of being shanghaied like this another Saturday. So far, because he was the "new kid," the other surgeons had deliberately kept him out of the rotation as an act of kindness on their part, but having been there a month now, he wasn't *that* new. And if it got him out of traipsing around stores, looking at furniture that made no impression on him—one piece was as good, or as bad, as another—so much the better.

Madelyn glanced down at the tips of her shoes, stoically bearing what seemed like a rejection. But Meghan was feistier than her sister and met her father's words head-on.

"Don't you like being with us, Daddy?" she asked.

The question caught him off guard. So much so that for a moment, his brain scrambled about for a way to answer the question with a dignity that would still allow him to avoid hurt feelings.

"Yes, of course I do, but—"

There was no room for a disclaimer. Taking her opportunity, Kennon instantly broke in, saying, "You live in the house as a family, you should all have a say in how it's decorated, even if each bedroom is that family member's personal…kingdom." She was going to say domain but she wasn't sure if the girls would understand that. "Think of it as a bonding experience," Kennon coaxed him.

Simon had to force himself to look away from her mouth. Another reason to try to distance himself from these Saturday excursions. He was spending too much time with this woman, allowing her to get under his skin, something she seemed to be able to accomplish even when they were in a crowd.

If he bonded more with any of them, in his opinion, he would need superglue remover. "I think we've bonded already."

She smiled, a flash of sympathy in her eyes. The good doctor was not unlike a lot of men when it came to shopping, but since this was so important to his girls—and helpful to her—she wasn't about to willingly let him off the hook. In her heart, she knew he couldn't mind *that* much. If he minded, he wouldn't be coming along. Simon Sheffield didn't strike her as the kind of man who did *anything* he didn't want to do.

"There's not all that much more of the house to do," she promised him, then added, "once you find a bedroom set you like."

The words *like* and *dislike* really had no meaning or importance to him when they were applied to something like furniture. Disinterested, Simon still knew better than to tell her to pick for him. She'd only send the ball back into his court, along with a lengthy lecture about building memories or something like that. Better to just give in and go.

Finally finishing the serving of pancakes that Edna had placed before him—predominantly with no memory of the actual act of eating—Simon got off the stool.

He sighed, resigned. "All right, let's get this over with."

"Your displeasure would sound a lot more believable if you weren't smiling," Kennon whispered to him as she passed by, herding the girls out before her.

"I'm not smiling," he protested, raising his voice so that it would carry out to her.

"'Fraid you are, sir," Edna confirmed quietly as she approached and collected the plates from the counter. She gave him an amused look just as he walked out of the kitchen.

Simon caught his reflection in the foyer mirror.

Damn, Kennon was right. He was smiling and he wasn't even aware of it. It *was* getting so that he couldn't depend on anyone, he thought darkly.

Not even himself.

A long, contented sigh escaped Kennon's lips.

She was exhausted, but happy. The day had turned out to be extralong, but it was definitely worth it. She felt exhilarated, because she felt she'd accomplished a great deal today.

She was not as confident as she pretended to be about getting him to put a stamp of approval on a complete bedroom set and actually mean it. But the shop she had brought Simon and the girls to had so many different selections that if they hadn't found something there, she would have been tempted to finally throw in the towel and admit that they would never find his furniture.

But there was no need for surrender. Simon had *found* something he actually liked.

As it turned out, Dr. Sheffield had been won over by a bedroom suite reminiscent of early California furniture. Massive and powerful looking, the set, surprisingly, was not all dark wood and oppression. While not light, the hue of the wood was somewhere in between the two extremes. A compromise of light and dark.

Seeing it, and Simon's reaction to it—his interest was actually piqued—led Kennon to believe that the bedroom suite was a great deal like Simon himself.

The man had a dark exterior, but underneath—when he would allow someone to experience that side of him— something within was lighter, more sensitive than first met the eye.

She just had to keep scratching at his dark surface to bring it out—for the girls' sake, she silently emphasized, since ultimately it was his daughters who had to live with the man. After this assignment was over, in all likelihood she would never see Simon Sheffield again. So whether or not he learned how to unwind, how to allow his softer, kinder side to come through, made no difference to her.

The hell it doesn't, a small voice whispered in her head as Kennon automatically glanced in a mirror that was mounted on the dining room wall.

She'd never cared for lies. Why was she lying to herself now?

The answer was simple. It was a matter of self-preservation. Because she was really attracted to Simon and she knew it wouldn't lead anywhere. He had his work and his daughters. And his heart belonged to his late wife. There was absolutely no room in his life for anything else. If she entertained even so much as a glimmer of a hope, she was an even bigger idiot than she'd been when Pete had walked out on her, leaving her with a bruised ego and a bleeding heart.

It was time to go home, she told herself. Her work was definitely done for the day. But as she prepared to leave, Edna gave her a sympathetic once-over.

"You look tired, Miss Cassidy. Why don't you stay awhile, catch your second wind? Stay for dinner. Have a nice cup of tea while you wait—you can put your feet up on that new hassock you and the doctor picked out," Edna added.

The hassock. The woman made it sound as if shopping had been a mutual experience. But it hadn't been. If ever there was a reluctant shopper, it was Simon Sheffield. And it was her job to get him to pick things out. She was getting paid, in effect, to pressure him.

"I think I'll have to pass." She glanced in Simon's direction. He was on the sofa, his eyes shut. Apparently she and the girls had completely tired him out. "I'm sure that Dr. Sheffield would like nothing better than to get me out of his hair for the evening," Kennon said with a small, disparaging laugh.

And probably for longer than that, she added silently.

A deep voice rose from his side of the room. "No hurry."

Startled, Kennon all but did a double take. The man made her jumpy, she realized. For oh, so many reasons. "I thought you were asleep," she told him.

"Apparently I'm not," he contradicted. Sitting up, he rotated his shoulders, shrugging off the tension that harnessed them. "Why don't you take Edna up on her offer of tea? And dinner," he added. "Unless, of course, you have plans."

He was actually asking her to hang out with them? Or had they somehow slipped into an alternate universe? "No," she managed to murmur. "No plans."

"All right, then it's settled," he told her. "Dinner and tea, not necessarily in that order."

Even the smallest feather would have succeeded in knocking her over with absolutely no effort at all.

Chapter Nine

"Here, dear, the tea as promised." Edna placed an oversize mug in Kennon's hands. "It's chai tea," she told the young woman. "Helps relax you," she added with a smile.

"What will relax me," Kennon said, already getting up off the stool where she had been planted only minutes ago, "is to help out with dinner."

"Me, too," Meghan chimed in, mimicking Kennon's tone.

"I want to help, too," Madelyn immediately protested.

Edna laughed quietly. "I am reminded of that old saying about too many cooks spoiling the soup," she said, her glance taking in all three of them.

"But it doesn't apply here," Kennon was quick to assure her.

"I was just about to say that," Edna agreed, an amused smile curving her lips.

It wasn't long before Edna was ushered off to a chair, to sit on the sidelines as an observer in her own domain. "I feel like a bump on a log, sitting here," she complained to Kennon.

"A much loved, honored bump," Kennon assured her. Since she was here, she wanted to feel useful, and that meant taking some of the burden off the older woman. "You do double duty as their nanny and the housekeeper, as well as the chief cook. You deserve a little time off. Besides, I like cooking and the girls like helping me, right, girls?" She glanced to the duo for backup.

"Right." Meghan nodded her head with vigor.

"Right," Madelyn agreed, bobbing her own head up and down.

"See?" Kennon said to the nanny. In her opinion, she'd just won her argument. "So you just sit back and relax. We'll do all the heavy lifting."

"What are we lifting?" Meghan asked, looking around the kitchen.

By now, Madelyn had caught on to Kennon-speak. "That's just another figure of speech, stu— Meggie," Madelyn abruptly switched gears, refraining from calling her sister stupid when Kennon gave her a warning look. "Right, Kennon?"

"Right," Kennon agreed, taking a large pot from the cabinet. Her own pots were back home again. This set of cast-iron, green pans were all brand-new, waiting to be broken in, one by one.

Meghan pouted for a moment, then tossed her head, her curls bouncing along her back as she declared, "I knew that."

Kennon smiled warmly at her smaller assistant. "Of

course you did. All right, troops, let's get this show on the road."

"I know, another 'figger of speech,'" Meghan announced knowingly with a smirk directed at her sister. She was more than eager to be pressed into service.

After a beat, Edna rose from the chair and crossed over to where her employer was sitting, still rifling through the paper.

"Warms your heart, doesn't it, sir?" she asked him in a lower voice.

Simon looked up from a rather sobering article on the current fate of lending institutions. Given her comment, he doubted the woman had been looking over his shoulder.

But just in case he'd misunderstood her, he asked, "What does?"

"The way Meghan and Madelyn have taken to her. Those girls light up like fireflies whenever they're around Miss Kennon. When she first came, I half expected them to be sullen and reject her, but they didn't. The poor lambs are hungry for a woman's touch."

They're not the only ones.

Where the hell had that come from, he wondered, startled by the stray thought that had just shot through his mind, triggered by Edna's comment.

Clearing his throat as he pulled himself together, Simon stated the obvious. "They have you."

"They've always had me, sir," Edna pointed out. "I've been part of their background ever since they were born. Just like you, sir," she said, looking at him significantly.

Was that a criticism of his failure to successfully connect with his daughters? When his wife first died, he'd withdrawn into himself, into a self-imposed exile of the soul until such time as he could breathe normally again, because, initially, he just couldn't. Couldn't breathe, couldn't cope, couldn't see himself living in a world without Nancy. But as one day fed into another and then another, and he was still standing, still drawing breath, he picked himself up and picked up the mantle of his responsibilities, as well. It wasn't easy, but he forced himself to return, to walk and talk, and dwell among the living. To dwell with his daughters, who needed him.

But connecting with them, well, that was something else again. That took time, patience and a know-how that he didn't naturally possess.

Reflecting on it now, Simon realized that he hadn't made as much headway in thirteen months as he had in these last four weeks. The difference being, he supposed he had to admit, that Kennon and her child-friendly manner had entered his life. He was more than willing to concede that the woman was special.

She would have had to be, he mused, since she had managed to somehow make shopping less than odious for him. Not an easy feat, he would be the first to admit.

He looked at Edna now, as the sound of his daughters' laughter drifted in from the kitchen. "I'm doing the best I can."

"I know that, sir, of course you are," Edna said soothingly. "But isn't it funny how Miss Cassidy makes that best better?" It was a statement rather than a question. "She's got a way about her, that one does." Edna smiled broadly. "I'm glad you found her."

"I didn't," he contradicted. "She found us. Or rather, she was sent to us."

Edna nodded solemnly, pleased that the doctor understood. "You feel that way, too, Doctor?"

He knew that Edna was thinking that the incredibly bubbly interior decorator's path crossed theirs by some sort of divine design, but the actual explanation was a great deal simpler.

"She was 'sent' by the woman who sold me the house, Edna," he clarified. Since Edna had been very ill at the time, he didn't really expect her to remember exactly how Kennon had initially burst into their lives and where she'd come from.

From the head of Zeus, he couldn't help thinking, being reminded of a story he'd read in a high school English class eons ago, back when life was far less complicated and happiness was not an elusive entity that came with a dark underbelly.

"You mean Maizie Sommers?" Edna asked. He was surprised that she remembered the Realtor's name. When he nodded, Edna said, "I must remember to send the woman a thank-you note for that referral. I doubt if anyone else than Miss Cassidy could have served up this miracle."

"And what miracle would that be?" he asked, completely clueless.

"Why, getting you to take the girls on a shopping trip these last few Saturdays," she said, surprised that the doctor didn't immediately realize what she was talking about.

"I didn't take the girls, the girls took me," Simon corrected.

And that had been because the woman who was now chopping celery and carrots with abandonment and relish had taken his daughters along with her. He wasn't familiar with the process, but he had a feeling that most decorators operated autonomously, at times sending their clients to stores on their own, or perhaps bringing things to them for their stamp of approval. A *rubber* stamp of approval.

He sincerely doubted that the decorating process that most people went through was as—for lack of a better word—*intimate* as the one he and the girls were experiencing.

"Even better," Edna was saying in response to his description.

He supposed it was better in a way. On his own he would have continued the way he'd been, making minor attempts to interact with his daughters, but for the most part, abdicating that position to Edna, who after all was far better at it than he was. Edna wouldn't have tried to get him to interact more with Madelyn and Meghan. She might have wanted to, but Edna was not the pushy type. Definitely not the way this woman with the sexy smile was.

As all these thoughts went through his mind and struck him with a numbing clarity for the first time, he felt like a man who had just experienced an epiphany.

Maybe the word *miracle* wasn't too strong after all.

Simon Sheffield had been looking at her all through dinner. Staring at her, really, Kennon silently amended, and she felt a little uneasy about it. Not to mention in-credibly warm.

Why was he staring?

What was he thinking?

Since he wasn't a man who could be easily read, she

couldn't help wondering if perhaps the doctor was trying to tell her that her services were no longer required.

No, that wasn't it. If he wanted to terminate her, he'd come right out and say it instead of playing cat-and-mouse games with her.

But he wouldn't just let her go while his daughters were at the table. Anyone with even an abbreviated attention span could tell that they had all but adopted her as one of their own. If Dr. Sheffield told her she didn't need to come back anymore while the girls were within earshot, they'd put up a heart-wrenching fuss, God love 'em. And although he wasn't exactly a candidate for father of the year, Simon Sheffield did love his daughters. She'd picked up on that almost from the very beginning. He just didn't know how to express it properly.

So was he just biding his time, waiting for the girls to go off and play?

Or was something else on his mind? Some other reason why he was looking at her like that, as if he was trying to find the hidden entrance to a building.

Had she committed some minor offense that had somehow snowballed in his mind? Or—?

Or what?

What was wrong with her? Why was all this tension, this anxiety wound up around this one man? It wasn't as if her livelihood depended on this one assignment. She wasn't exactly going to be penniless and on the street when this job was over. And it would be over, if not now, then in a few weeks. Everything ended sooner or later.

But that was the nature of the beast. She came, she saw, she decorated. And then she left. She always left. It was the one constant, the one thing that never changed, even when all the other variables did.

So why did she feel this resistance to having things end? Now or later, it shouldn't matter.

And yet, it did.

All the reasoning in the world didn't help her wrestle this anxious feeling that insisted on weaving itself through her, anchoring her to the ground. It just kept threatening to overwhelm her.

She didn't want this time with Simon and his daughters to end, she realized. She didn't want it to be over. But she couldn't stretch it out indefinitely. The whole point of it was to get it finished quickly. That's what Simon wanted. To have his house decorated and to be as little involved in the process as humanly possible.

Too late for that wish to be granted.

The problem was that in getting him involved she'd managed, quite unintentionally, to get herself involved, as well.

The moment dinner was over, Kennon was on her feet, ready to clear the dishes so that she could also clear the air and finally ask Simon why he kept looking at her like that. It had kept her from eating—and from tasting any of the little bit that she *had* put in her mouth.

But even as she began gathering up the plates, Edna reached over and took them from her, saying, "You cooked, we'll clean." She looked down at the pint-size cheering squad that flanked her. "Won't we, girls?"

This time, there was a display of reluctance on the part of the junior league helpers.

Meghan put it into words first. "Can't we stay with Kennon?"

"Miss Cassidy," Edna said, deliberately being formal in hopes that the girls would follow suit, "has earned the right to sit this out, girls. You, however, are both still filled with energy. Energy I can put to very good use," Edna told them.

Meghan's lower lip stuck out a full inch beyond her upper one as she pouted to show her disappointment and frustration.

"Tell you what, you listen to Edna," Kennon coaxed, wanting to avoid any flare-ups, "and next Saturday, we'll take a little break from shopping."

Madelyn was quick to put two and two together. She didn't appear to much like four. "Take a break?" she asked, her tone distressed. "Does that mean you won't come over?"

"No." Kennon was quick to put the older girl's mind at ease. "That means that I'm going to take you two to an amusement park right here in Orange County—" She glanced over toward Simon. "As long as your dad says it's all right," she added.

"Can we, Dad?" Meghan immediately began begging. "Can we go?"

"Please, Dad? We haven't been to one yet and Mom always promised that if we were ever down here, we could go."

Rather than answer his daughters' pleas, he glanced at Kennon, a hint of surprise in his eyes. "You don't want me to go with you?" This was certainly a change, Simon thought. Instead of feeling like he had just gotten off the hook, he felt oddly disappointed.

Kennon had to admit that the question completely stunned her. If she'd been a betting woman, she would have wagered that Simon would be relieved that she wasn't pushing for him to come along. Not the reverse.

"Well, yes, of course." Brightening, she was honest

with him. "But I thought that might be too much to hope for." Obviously not. She took a deep breath. "So, do you want to come with us?"

Playing hard-to-get at this point would be ridiculous. That ship had come and gone. "Sure, why not?"

"Why not, indeed," Edna chimed in from the kitchen doorway, looking incredibly pleased with this twist of events.

"Oh, yes, you, too, Edna," Kennon called out, belatedly realizing that she had neglected to include the woman, as well. Even nannies needed to kick back and relax once in a while. "You're invited, too. My treat," she added. Turning back to Simon, she clasped her hands together. "Okay, so it's settled—" About to fling herself into the next part of this dialogue, she was thrown off base when Simon interrupted.

"No, it's not," he contradicted.

"Oh?" Well, that peace treaty was short-lived, she thought.

"It's not settled because it's going to be my treat," he informed her. "I can afford it a lot more than you can—unless you're really drastically overcharging me," he slipped in. "And making a bundle that way."

He didn't expect her to answer, or to challenge what he said. But even when she agreed with him, it sounded as if she was disagreeing.

"No, I'm not overcharging you," she replied. "Or making a bundle. I'm going out of my way to find you the best deals, the best prices—"

"I know, I know. Uncle," he cried. "I conceded the point, no need to keep heaping words on my head."

She had more words for him. She wanted him to tell

her why he'd been looking at her that way all through dinner.

As if sensing that this was not over, Edna came in to gather up her stray workers. "All right, girls, dishes, remember?" Edna reminded them.

Scrambling off their chairs, the girls were quick to do as they were told—without any further objections. That was a thing of the past as excitement seemed to shine in their eyes.

They were definitely thinking about next Saturday.

"You made them very happy," she said to their father once they were finally alone.

"Wasn't my idea, it was yours."

"It was my idea for me to take them to an amusement park," she clarified so that he wouldn't wind up missing the point. "They're excited because you're coming with us. With them," she corrected herself. "*That's* the important part."

He looked at her for a long moment, choosing his words slowly, debating not saying them at all, because in not speaking he would remain safe. But once he spoke, Simon knew he wasn't going to be safe anymore. Reason would dictate him saying nothing. But reason wasn't the leader right now.

His voice disrupted the temporary silence that had seeped in. "Actually, I think the important part in all this is you."

The man was setting a record tonight in how many times he could stun her. "Me?" she asked incredulously.

Simon couldn't help himself. He had to laugh. "You do innocent well—for a devious person."

She squared her shoulders in a defensive manner she wasn't aware of. But he took note of the action.

"I'm not devious," she protested.

Simon didn't back off. He wasn't out for an argument. If anything, he was out for the exact opposite. "Yes, you are. But fortunately, you use your powers for good." And then he saw Kennon grinning—not smiling, but grinning—at him. Why? "What?" he asked.

"I just can't picture you saying what you just said," she told him.

He had to agree with her. He couldn't picture himself cracking a joke. She'd done that, had made him unearth a lighter side of himself. "And yet I did," he said.

"Yes, you did."

For a moment, she just studied him. Something stirred within her. Pride? No, it felt as if it was more than that. But she'd settle for the word until a better one came along.

"You've come a long way from that brusque cardio-vascular surgeon I met at the front door a month ago," she told him.

The fact that he didn't immediately protest her assumption told him that she was right. He had come a long way—without realizing that he was making the transition.

"I guess I have," he conceded. His eyes met hers and held for more than a beat. "And it's all your doing."

She frowned thoughtfully. "I can't quite tell if you're thanking me or blaming me."

"Then maybe I should try to make myself a little clearer," he suggested.

It was hard to tell who was more surprised by what happened next, him or the woman who had covertly led him down this path he'd had absolutely no intention of taking.

Until he did.

One moment he was sitting at the dining room table, trying to sort everything out for once by verbalizing his thoughts, the next he was leaning over that same table, framing her face with his surgeon's hands. Hands that were capable of doing the most delicate of surgeries, but now felt almost large and clumsy to him as he took the next unforeseen step.

Simon found himself kissing her.

Chapter Ten

If Simon felt any regret over what he was doing, for the moment it was hidden behind large, heavy drapes that had been drawn back in order to admit the sun, the warmth that existed outside the dwelling he'd exiled himself to so many months ago.

Right now, he was caught up in the moment. Caught up in the very fact that he could feel.

He'd thought that ability had been lost to him.

His mind reeled.

How could something so soft, so delicate have such a powerful kick?

Simon had no answer. All he knew was that Kennon's kiss, begun in surprise with a touch like a butterfly landing on a rose petal, grew in strength and magnitude until it was all encompassing. It was as if nothing existed outside its realm.

Simon rose from his chair, his hands on her upper

arms as he drew her up to her feet with him. He wanted to be closer to her, without a damn table between them like some kind of impeding obstacle.

And all the while, his lips remained on hers. And her soft mouth remained on his.

He couldn't begin to describe what was going on inside of him. It felt as if a shaft of light had shattered the oppressive darkness, laying claim to all of him.

Having brought her up to her feet, he pulled Kennon to him, holding her as if, at any moment, she would melt and slide through his fingers.

From the first moment she'd met Simon she'd had a feeling he was capable of this, of setting her on fire with just the touch of his lips to hers.

But *feeling* and *knowing* were two very different things.

She'd seriously underestimated just how powerfully he could rock her foundations. It was true that she hadn't been with anyone, hadn't so much as exchanged a quick, friendly kiss with a man since Pete had shattered her world and sent her self-esteem on a one-way trip to nowhere. That had been more than a little while ago.

Even so, she knew the difference between nice and teeth-jarring. Between okay and wonderfully soul-inspiring. And Simon Sheffield with his mind-blowing mouth definitely fell into the latter category.

Thankfully when he finally drew back, he was still holding on to her arms. If he hadn't been, she had more than a passing suspicion that she would have found herself unceremoniously sinking to the floor.

With her lips no longer hermetically sealed to his, Kennon had to concentrate on catching her breath. It felt as if she had just completed a twenty-six-mile marathon inside of a time warp. Her head was spinning badly. It was a huge effort to get her mind back in gear, because right now rainbows and fireworks had taken over.

And she wanted to kiss him again.

Damn it, get hold of yourself. You're not some starry-eyed teenager—and neither is he.

But that was just the problem. She *did* feel starry-eyed. And the racing pulse, the sweaty palms, the shortness of breath, they *all* belonged to a naive, inexperienced teenager.

What had he done to her?

Blowing out a long breath, she drew an even longer one in. Desperate to divert his attention from what she assumed was her flushed face, Kennon said the first thing she could think of.

"I guess this means you're thanking me," she said, referring to the last words that had left her mouth before the world as she knew it had burnt to a crisp.

"Something like that," Simon agreed, his tone deliberately evasive.

Think, Kennon, think. Form sentences, don't just stand there like some kind of village idiot. He'll think you've never been kissed before.

Well, she hadn't. Not like this. Not *ever* like this.

Her brain took baby steps, searching for a subject. And then she found one, thank goodness.

"About the amusement park," Kennon began haltingly, reverting back to the only topic that even marginally occurred to her. The rest of her mind was a charred wasteland.

"You change your mind about going?" Simon asked, surprised.

Maybe after he'd broken all the unwritten rules by

kissing her, Kennon had decided to avoid any additional complications by bailing on her initial suggestion. Not that he could blame her. He wasn't sure just what had come over him, except that for a single moment he'd wanted to be human again, wanted to know if he was *capable* of being human again.

Obviously he was and he could—apparently all too well.

He'd probably scared her, he realized. He sure as hell had scared himself. And yet, despite all that, despite crossing lines he knew he shouldn't have for a myriad of reasons, he felt like smiling. Smiling because, just for the length of that incredible encounter, he'd not only felt human, there'd been this glimmer of hope inside him. But even as he became aware of it, he could feel it fade with the stab of disloyalty, of guilt.

He had no right to reach for happiness, no right to *be* happy. Because Nancy couldn't be happy. Because Nancy had died in his place.

"No." Did he want her to change her mind? But she couldn't. Once she'd made the suggestion, she couldn't go back on it. The girls would be heartbroken. "I just wanted to tell you which park I thought the girls—and you—might like to go to."

Her voice sounded tinny to her ear. She stumbled, looked for words to hold back the silence that threatened to devour them. And as she looked up at Simon, she could see the happiness receding in his eyes. Worse, she could see what rose in his eyes to take its place. A sadness that tore at her soul.

She didn't want to have him withdraw before she got to explore what had just happened here.

Don't feel bad about this. Please don't feel bad about this.

She cleared her throat, hoping that her voice wouldn't crack as she spoke. "I thought that maybe Knott's Berry Farm might be fun for them." She realized that it sounded as if she was calling all the shots so she added, "Unless you have a better idea."

He didn't have a better idea. He didn't have an idea at all. He was still a little punchy, a little groggy from the impact of what they had just shared. What he had just started without thinking it through.

"No," he murmured. "I don't have a better idea. Knott's Berry Farm's fine. I'm sure that the girls'll love it."

Because apparently they love you.

He realized that Edna was right. The girls were desperate for a woman's attention. And they had picked their woman.

He couldn't complain that they had bad taste. Their taste was right on the money—and it bothered him that he thought that, but he did.

"Good." Kennon caught her lower lip between her teeth, thinking. Debating. And before she knew it, she heard herself asking, "Are you all right, Doctor?"

It seemed ridiculous to call him by his title after he'd kissed her hard enough to knock the socks off her bare feet, but she didn't want him to think that things had changed between them.

Even though they had.

"I'm—" Simon was about to say *fine,* but then he thought better of it. "Actually, I'm not sure."

A wariness entered her eyes. He wanted her to understand. Understand that he wasn't trying to take advantage of her, or attempting to set the stage for a future, more heated encounter. This had just *happened*, without any deliberate premeditation on his part.

He needed her to know that. "Kennon, I'm still trying to get over things—I'm still trying to realign my day-to-day world and make sense out of it." It was hard for him to admit this, hard to share something so personal. "My wife was a huge part of everything about me."

She wondered what it felt like, to be loved that way. Cherished that way. But to put him at ease, she nodded and said, "I understand."

He still wasn't certain that he had made things right. "If I gave you the wrong idea—"

Now, what did *that* mean? Was he sorry he'd kissed her? Or just sorry if she thought he was forcing himself on her in a minor way? Just what was the "wrong" idea—and what was the right one?

"No, no wrong idea," she told him brightly, doing her best to seem as if she was making light of the whole situation. "No ideas at all," she emphasized. "You know, like that song in *Casablanca* said, 'a kiss is just a kiss'."

Although she knew that she felt a follow-up would have been more than a little nice, maybe this was for the best after all. No complications for him, and she wouldn't run the very real risk of feeling like a fool once it was over.

"It's not like I'm expecting to find roses scattered all over my store," she added, tongue in cheek.

When she pressed her lips together, she could still taste him. Her pulse jumped. Okay, it was time to retreat before she gave in to the desire to kiss him again.

"I think I'd better be going. I do have some things to

catch up on," she added, hoping he didn't think it was as lame an excuse as it sounded.

Simon nodded. "I guess we were monopolizing your time."

Even though it gave her a way out, she couldn't let him think that was how she felt. It added a negative edge to things that just wasn't true.

But coming on too strong might give him the wrong idea, too. So she kept her tone light as she told him, "That would only be a problem if I minded being monopolized." Then, in case the man harbored even a kernel of a doubt, she assured him, with feeling, "I don't."

Reaching for her purse, she slipped the strap onto her shoulder and began to head for the door. He fell into step beside her. That was when she heard the sound of two pairs of feet, running quickly and heading in her direction.

"You're leaving?" Madelyn cried, dismayed, her lower lip protruding just a little.

"Without saying goodbye?" The accusation came from Meghan.

"It's just until Monday," Kennon told them as she cupped Meghan's chin in her hand. If she ever had daughters, she'd want them to be just like this—

Hold it, don't get started down this path, she warned herself.

Right now, there were no daughters on her horizon. She had a business to run and a profit to turn. Beyond that, her most complicated endeavor should be deciding which movie to put into the Blu-ray player. She'd promised herself a break from men, from thinking of them in any other light than as potential clients.

Her heart just wasn't ready to undertake another journey down Niagara Falls.

But if it had been, a little voice inside her head whispered, Simon Sheffield would have definitely been right up there as a leading candidate to bring the journey to fruition.

"Can't you come by tomorrow, Kennon?" Meghan asked.

Simon came to her rescue. "Give the poor woman a break, Meghan. Seeing the two of you seven days would be above and beyond the call of duty. You guys are more than a handful," he told them, draping an arm around each girl's shoulders.

Meghan wiggled free, her eyes on Kennon. "But we like seeing you seven days a week," she told the woman she'd decided was her new best friend. And then she looked over at her older sister, clearly asking for backup. She received it readily.

"If you don't want to come over here, can we go over to your house tomorrow?" Madelyn asked hopefully.

Simon appeared stunned at his daughter's question. "Madelyn, you don't just invite yourself over to someone's house," he chided.

The little hurt face was just more than Kennon could bear. Besides, she had no plans for Sunday other than sleeping in late. She gave Madelyn a warm, encouraging smile. "Sure, you can see it," she told her. "If Edna doesn't mind bringing you."

"Sunday's Edna's day off," Madelyn said. A fighter, she wasn't about to accept defeat easily. "But Dad can bring us, can't you, Dad?"

Kennon didn't want to put Simon on the spot. But she would have been lying to herself if she pretended that

she didn't want to hear his answer. Now that the idea
had been presented, she would really love to see him
on her own home territory.

So rather than volunteer to swing by and pick the
girls up herself, Kennon waited to hear what he had to
say.

Caught off guard by his daughter's request, it took
him a moment to answer. When he finally did and said,
"Sure, I can bring them," Kennon felt something inside
grow warm, spreading out to all parts of her, along with
a tingling sensation.

Quickly writing down her address on a piece of paper,
she handed it to him. "How does eleven o'clock sound
to you?" she asked.

The question was for Simon, but it was Meghan who
answered, declaring, "It sounds perfect!"

Both girls were grinning from ear to ear.

"Then it's all settled. I'll see you tomorrow," she
said.

Turning on her heel, she walked quickly away before
Simon had a chance to declare his previous response
null and void. As she closed the front door behind her,
she caught herself humming.

Kennon heard her cell phone ringing in her purse as
she drove home. She stifled her urge to reach for it and
answer the call. But because she hadn't mounted the
phone on its stand on the dashboard or activated her
Bluetooth before starting up the car, she had to let the
call go to voice mail. Doing so drove her crazy as well
as set her curiosity into high gear.

There was nothing she could do about it without
risking a fine should a policeman suddenly materialize

behind her. California frowned on cell phones and hands making contact while driving anywhere.

Ten minutes later, the cell phone rang again just as she entered her development. Her curiosity swelled another notch, tempting her to at least sneak a peek at who the caller was. That was when she saw him. A motorcycle policeman taking the major cross street right where she'd turned into the development. The cell phone remained where it was.

When her cell phone rang a third time, just as she put her key into the lock on her front door, Kennon could finally indulge her curiosity. She paused to dig through her purse to retrieve the phone. It took her a minute, despite the fact that she'd stripped down her purse to what she felt were the bare essentials.

Locating the device, she flipped it open and let herself into her house. It was too dark to see the caller's name on the tiny screen. Kennon felt around for the light switch. "Hello?"

"Well, it's about time. If it hadn't been for that eighteen hours of labor I suffered through, I would have started thinking that maybe I'd made you up."

Kennon suppressed a sigh. Finding the light switch, she turned it on as she closed the door with her back. "Hello, Mother."

"Ah, you remember who I am, that's encouraging. But you've obviously forgotten my phone number, and where I live. I haven't heard from you in eons, much less actually seen you. Have you changed much? Would I still be able to recognize you if I saw you across the street?"

It hadn't been that long. She'd seen her mother just before she'd taken on this assignment. Her mother had always liked to exaggerate. Ruth Cassidy had a flair for the melodramatic.

"Sorry." Kennon apologized because she knew her mother expected her to. "It's been a little hectic lately."

"Good hectic or bad hectic?" her mother pressed.

She hated getting the third degree, but she supposed that, since she was her mother's only child, there was no getting around it. Maybe, if she were in that same position, a divorced mother of an adult child, she'd feel the same way.

"Good hectic," Kennon told her. "I've been working closely with a client." Actually more closely with his daughters, she added silently, but her mother didn't need to hear that. She knew how her mother's mind worked. It leaped from one conclusion to another, creating a completely impossible fantasy scenario out of the tiniest bits and pieces.

"What kind of a client?" her mother was asking.

Oh, God, she'd woken the sleeping giant.

"The kind who needs to have his whole house decorated," she answered, praying that would be the end of it. Knowing it wouldn't.

The answer seemed to satisfy her mother. Hope sprang eternal. And then it died the next moment. "Then he's wealthy. Good, good. Anything else you want to tell me?" her mother coaxed.

Right now she didn't want to tell her mother even this much because she knew the way her mother thought. Ruth Cassidy wanted nothing more than to have her only daughter, her only *child,* walk down the aisle and promise to love, honor and cherish a man in a rented tuxedo. And if he was a rich man in his own tuxedo, so much the better.

Well, at least there were no surprises there. Her mother had been making noises about her "finding someone" from the moment Kennon had graduated high school and subsequently gone off to college.

"Anything else," Kennon echoed. "Yes, my feet hurt and I'm tired. Can I call you back, Mother?" *Like, in another month or so?*

"Of course you *can*," her mother answered, sounding a little miffed. "But whether you will or not is a whole other story." That was definitely the sound of complaining in her mother's voice, Kennon thought. "You know, I'm not going to live forever."

Uh-uh, here we go again. The guilt trip. Not tonight, Mother. I'm exhausted.

"Of course you are, Mom. God's not ready to have you come up and rearrange heaven on him. You just might wind up being the first woman who lives pretty close to forever."

She heard her mother sigh deeply on the other end. "Oh, 'how sharper than a serpent's tooth—'"

About to open the refrigerator to get a can of diet soda, Kennon rolled her eyes. She'd been hearing this particular quote from *King Lear* since before she'd hit her teens.

"'It is to have a thankless child,' uh-huh, yes, I know. I promise, Mom, if you give me a kingdom, I won't turn you out. You can even have your pick of towers." *If you promise to stay there.* "But right now, I'm really beat and I still need to clean up—"

The second she said it, she knew she had made a

tactical mistake and could have bitten off her tongue. Her only hope was that her mother hadn't heard.

"Why do you need to clean up?"

Hope went down in flames. "Because I'm having company over tomorrow." She hated being faced with a long list of things to do first thing in the morning.

Her mother was quick to volunteer helpful advice. "Your Aunt Maizie's got that friend with the cleaning service. I can get the number from her and you could give them a call—"

Evening stretched out before them. "Mom, my company's coming tomorrow at eleven," she said, stubbornly not putting a name to her "company." "There's not enough time for someone to—"

"Leave it to me. There's *always* enough time," her mother promised.

Again Kennon rolled her eyes. Why did she even bother arguing? "Mom, I'm not about to throw away money on something I can do myself."

"You sound exhausted. You're always edgy when you're exhausted. You need your sleep, baby."

Kennon knew it was futile to point out that it had been a long time since she had actually qualified for that term. "Fine. I'll get up early tomorrow and clean then. Now, good night, Mom," she said firmly, adding, "I'll call you back later," to assuage her conscience.

She could have sworn she heard her mother say, "When pigs fly," but she wasn't about to respond. She didn't want to be drawn into another round only to arrive nowhere.

Chapter Eleven

Kennon had nothing against mornings. As long as they arrived at a reasonable hour, say, seven-thirty or so. When they began at six, the way hers had today, all bets were off.

Groping her way into the kitchen after her alarm had unceremoniously woken her up, Kennon found that her first challenge of the day was making herself a bracing cup of coffee. Her coordination was not the greatest before the sun actually occupied the sky. But without coffee, she knew she was not about to come to for at least another hour if not longer.

Setting her alarm for six had seemed like a pretty good idea last night. Not so much this morning. But then, she really did need to get up this early. Her house needed cleaning and she needed to get moving.

Soon.

The landline rang at five to seven, just after she'd

cleared away her coffee cup and what had passed for breakfast. She looked at the phone accusingly. It was too early for a wrong number, unless it was coming from another part of the country and, considering that she didn't know anyone from another part of the country, that wasn't exactly likely.

When it continued ringing, she reached for the receiver. "Hello?"

"Oh, good," she heard her mother's voice cheerfully declare, "you're up."

This had to qualify as penance somewhere, Kennon thought. "I had to get up, the phone was ringing," Kennon responded, her voice devoid of any kind of emotion or inflection.

"Very droll, dear. But you are up, right?" her mother asked.

"Yes, I'm up." *And feeling terrible,* she added silently. "But why would that matter to you?" she asked. Bits and pieces of her conversation with her mother last night came back to her. Was her mother giving her a wake-up call?

"Because I know you hate for me to use my key to get into your house."

That got her attention. Kennon was wide-awake and on her feet immediately. The last thing she wanted was her mother driving over here at this hour.

"Mother, you don't need to use the key," Kennon told her.

She heard her mother sigh. "But breaking down the door is so melodramatic, dear. We'd only have to put it up again, and repairing it would use up too much precious time."

"'We'?" Kennon echoed incredulously. "Who's 'we'?" she demanded.

Rather than words, the sound of the doorbell ringing was her answer. Taking a deep fortifying breath, Kennon made her way over to the front door and opened it, hoping for a burglar.

Her hopes were dashed.

"We are, dear," Ruth Cassidy said, smiling broadly as she gestured about. Kennon found herself looking at her mother, her aunt Maizie and another, stately, pleasant-faced woman, all of whom stood right outside her threshold. "This is Cecilia Parnell, one of your aunt Maizie's dearest friends," her mother announced, nodding toward the woman on her left. "We've come to get your house ready," she added, sweeping in with the aplomb of a woman who was accustomed to taking charge.

Kennon turned toward her aunt, hoping that she could appeal to the woman's common sense.

"It's not being photographed by *Architectural Digest*. There's no need to 'get it ready.' I'm just having a man and his two daughters over." This huge slip of the tongue she could blame on the fact that she was still sleepy and not thinking clearly—but then, when it came right down to it, her mother had that sort of effect on her all too often.

"Oh, so he's the one coming over." Ruth's wide smile grew even wider—and even more satisfied looking.

As if you haven't already figured that out, Kennon thought. She knew that her back was against the wall and the sooner she verified the fact for her mother, the sooner this cat-and-mouse game would be over.

"The girls wanted to see my house. I said fine. Come

at eleven. They're coming. End of story," she said in a clipped economy of words.

Rather than say anything to her daughter, Ruth looked over at her former sister-in-law. "You see what I have to put up with?" It was a dramatically intoned question, ending with a deep, soul-wrenching sigh.

In response, Maizie gazed at her late brother's daughter and patted Kennon's cheek. "Don't worry, dear, we'll be out of your hair before you know it. Just relax, we'll take care of everything."

How could she relax with hot-and-cold mature women running about her house? "But I don't need you to clean my house, Aunt Maizie. Please, I can do this myself," Kennon insisted.

There was actually sympathy in Maizie's eyes and, for one bright, shining moment, Kennon believed she'd won. But the moment passed as soon as Maizie opened her mouth to speak.

"No offense, dear, but Cecilia can do it better. It's what she does—quickly and thoroughly," Maizie assured her niece. Then she looked at Ruth and slipped her arm through the other woman's arm. "C'mon, we're going to need you."

A bit puzzled, Ruth looked from Maizie to her daughter. She hadn't come to work. "But I thought I'd just talk to Kennon—"

"Sorry, you thought wrong." Maizie hustled her toward the stairs. "If you're very good, Cecilia's going to let you use the vacuum cleaner upstairs—"

"There's no need to clean upstairs," Kennon protested, following in their wake. "Everyone's going to stay down here."

The look Maizie gave her seemed to marvel at her

naiveté. "They're eight and six," she reminded her niece. "They move around, explore, all while you're sitting on the sofa, confident that they haven't budged. We'll clean upstairs. Besides, you never know how things might turn out…"

She allowed her voice to trail off, ushered out by a smile that would have been called mischievous if the woman had been forty-five years younger. "Go, take a hot bubble bath. Relax. We'll take care of everything."

That was when the doorbell rang again.

This was beginning to feel like an Amtrak station in the middle of Los Angeles, Kennon thought, irritated, as she went to the door again. She opened it to find another woman she didn't recognize. This one appeared to be around the same age as her mother, her aunt and the woman they'd brought to clean her house.

"Ah, you must be Kennon," the newest invader said warmly.

"I must be," Kennon agreed, doing her best not to sound unfriendly—or annoyed. "And you're part of my mother's posse?"

"More like part of Maizie's," the quietly attractive woman confided. "I'm Theresa."

The next moment, Theresa Manetti was carrying in a rather large covered tray. Stunned, Kennon turned around to see her mother ducking down the hall behind her aunt. *Not so fast, Mother.*

"Mother, what is going on?" she called out. She was afraid to find out who would turn up on her doorstep next. A gypsy violinist?

Ruth Cassidy did not make her way back. Only her voice was heard as she answered, "The rest of your life, I hope."

Kennon shook her head, momentarily accepting defeat. She went upstairs to get a hot shower and to hopefully wake up from this fantasy that had somehow invaded her brain.

By the time Kennon finally left the shelter of the hot shower and got dressed—in a room that looked infinitely better than it had when she'd shut the bathroom door behind her—she had the unmistakably eerie feeling that she was alone.

Had all of this been a fantasy the way she'd told herself it was?

She would have really bought into the idea that she'd just imagined all this, except for the fact that everything in her house was practically sparkling now.

How could four women who, while not old, had definitely seen some years go by, work so fast, Kennon wondered, stunned. Whatever vitamins they were taking, she most certainly needed to tap into their supply—and cut her mother's stash while she was at it.

Moving from room to room, Kennon looked about in absolute wonder. She couldn't remember the last time she'd seen everything so neat and tidy at the same time.

There was nothing left for her to do except get ready. That, and try to tame the butterflies that had made a sudden, unexpected appearance in the middle of her stomach.

This was absurd, Kennon lectured herself. There was no reason to feel nervous—and she wouldn't *be* nervous if it hadn't been for her mother making such a big deal out of all this.

If she hadn't come barreling in with her mop squad and cleaned up a storm.

Tidying up would have kept her busy and, Kennon felt, more importantly, kept her from thinking. Now there was nothing for her to do but think.

And answer the door, she thought as she heard the doorbell ring. She glanced at her watch. It was still early. Maybe that was her mother again, coming back with some kind of provocative outfit for her to wear and tempt Simon with, she thought sarcastically.

Most likely a G-string and pasties. Her mother was desperate. After all, Cousin Nikki had a man—and Kennon didn't. Her mother was nothing if not competitive when it came to things like that.

"Forget something?" Kennon asked as she swung open the door.

"Not that I know of," Simon answered. He was standing there, one hand on each of his daughter's shoulders. Most likely to hold them in place. The girls seemed ready to spring at her. "Did I?" he asked, his eyes traveling over the length of her.

His long, lingering glance told her he wasn't seeing her as his decorator, or even as the woman who had earned the adoration of his daughters. He was looking at her as if he was seeing her for the first time—and definitely liking what he saw.

"No," she replied, her mouth only slightly more moist than a box of three-day-old sawdust. "I, um, thought you were my mother. She just left."

He glanced over his shoulder toward the street. But there was no foot traffic to speak of. "Sorry I missed meeting her."

"No, you're not," Kennon assured him emphatically.

"Trust me, you're not," she added for good measure. She glanced down at the girls, feeling on more secure ground when she addressed them. "Hi, girls. I sure hope you came hungry, because there's enough food here to feed a squadron of people."

"You shouldn't have gone to all this trouble," Simon told her as he released his daughters. True to form. Madelyn and Meghan were across the threshold in an instant, looking around, absorbing everything.

Kennon knew that her mother would have wanted her to say something about it being no trouble at all, that she'd whipped this up on the spur of the moment, but she had always preferred the truth. Now was no exception.

"I didn't," she told him, closing the front door behind him. "My aunt has this friend whose cooking, I'm told, brings tears to your eyes."

"Heartburn?" Simon guessed, his face utterly straight.

It took her a second to realize that he was kidding. Kennon laughed, the tension, for the most part, mercifully draining from her. "No, apparently the woman is so good, she knows how to make a feast out of a twig and a medium-size napkin."

"Now *that* I'd like to see," he told her, his amusement apparent.

"And her other friend, as you can see—" Kennon gestured slowly about the room and the house beyond "—cleans up a storm."

Simon listened and nodded, though there was a bit of a skeptical glimmer in his eyes. "Are these your mother's friends, or your fairy godmothers?"

It did sound a little like a fairy tale, now that she

thought about it, Kennon acknowledged. "A little of both, I imagine. My mother thought I needed help in order to impress you."

When she said this, it was meant to be an all-encompassing *you,* but one look at his face told her that he'd taken the word in the singular sense.

"You don't need help for that," Simon assured her quietly.

Her skin both warmed and entertained a chill at the same time. It defied understanding, but then so did the look in his dark blue eyes. She had to remind herself to breathe.

"Can I see upstairs?" Meghan asked eagerly, unwittingly coming to her rescue. Kennon took the opportunity to pull herself together.

Simon was still trying to find his way in this maze called parenthood, looking for a golden mean that allowed him to be a disciplinarian without being an ogre. He tried to instill his voice with affection even as he made it stern, no easy feat.

"Meghan." He turned to look at his younger daughter. "What did I say about asking for things?"

"Don't," the little girl mumbled, dejected, as she kept her head down.

"That's all right," Kennon assured him. After Cecilia had swept through, she had nothing to hide, nothing to feel ashamed of. Every single last cobweb, as well as the spider responsible for it, had been sent packing. "Sure, you can go see upstairs." She gestured toward Madelyn to include her in the safari. "You all can."

"Dad, too?" Meghan wanted to know, showing her father a toothy grin as if to say that there were no hard feelings.

"Your dad, too," Kennon assured her.

Okay, so it *was* a good thing, she thought as she led the way upstairs, that Cecilia had decided to clean upstairs. She just fervently hoped she wouldn't be forced to admit that to her mother. Humble pie was not her favorite form of dessert, and her mother was not above crowing a little when things went her way.

It wasn't until they all came back downstairs again after the impromptu tour of the second floor that it suddenly struck Kennon. Someone was missing.

Edna.

She knew it was the woman's day off, but she'd thought the nanny would take the opportunity to come by anyway—as a friend. Had she had a relapse? Now that Kennon thought of it, Edna *had* been looking a little under the weather. The woman had never fully recovered from that time she'd come down with the flu.

"Where's Edna?" she asked Madelyn abruptly. "I thought that maybe she'd come along with you after all."

"She wanted to come but she got a phone call," Meghan volunteered.

Kennon looked at Simon over the tops of his daughters' heads. "Nothing bad, I hope."

That, he thought, was a matter of opinion. His was that it *was* bad, but not for the reason that someone might initially think. It was bad because it left him high and dry—and in need of a nanny.

"Her nephew's wife just gave birth to their first baby and she's come down with an extreme case of the jitters," he told Kennon. "Edna asked if she could take a few days off to help out. She sends her regrets," he added.

Meghan tugged on his jacket sleeve. "Is it catching?" she asked when he finally gave her his attention.

"No, it's not something one person can give to another," Simon answered. Meghan seemed relieved when she smiled her thanks.

She didn't know about that, Kennon thought. If what Simon maintained was true, then he wouldn't have made her feel so terribly jittery inside.

"When's she coming back?" she asked him for conversation's sake.

"She said Thursday—with any luck," Simon added. "In the meantime, I'm going to have to call the cardiovascular group tomorrow morning and have them move around my appointments," he said more to himself than to the woman he was talking to.

Kennon didn't quite follow him. "Why?"

He smiled indulgently. He'd discovered that the more he smiled, the more he was inclined to smile. Another revelation that Kennon was responsible for.

"Because as of yet I haven't found a way to be in two places at once, no matter how hard I try. I can't very well see patients and pick up the girls from school at the same time." It was June and ordinarily school would either be over or winding down for the summer. But he'd enrolled the girls in a year-round school, thinking it would be good for them.

Kennon could see how attempting to be in two places at once might be a problem for him. But the solution was easy enough.

"I'll pick them up for you," Kennon volunteered cheerfully. She liked the look of surprise that entered his eyes. Liked, too, the way it made her feel that she had put it there. "I already know where the school is and it's not like I have to put in eight hours behind a desk every day. I'm my own boss so I can arrange my schedule accordingly. I can also be there to pick them up from school."

Grateful though he was, that wasn't the end of the complications.

"I also need someone to stay with them until I get home. Do you know anyone who would be available for that?" he asked.

Actually, she did. Her mother. Her mother would be thrilled to babysit, but if Kennon made that suggestion to the woman, it would be tantamount to opening up a Pandora's box. She knew from past experiences that her mother was the type of person who, if you gave her an inch, she not only took a mile, but constructed a building on it and gave the property a fancy new name.

In the long run, Kennon felt that she would be better off just offering to pitch in herself. After all, it wasn't going to be an ongoing thing. It was just for a few days, and her decorating business wasn't exactly drowning in work at the moment.

The belt-tightening conditions of the present economy had been hard on everyone. Nathan was perfectly capable of running the shop for the next couple of days.

"Yes, I know someone. Me."

Simon looked at her skeptically, even as his daughters let out a gleeful cheer and lost no time in surrounding her.

"I can't ask you to do that," he protested.

"You didn't ask," Kennon pointed out. "I volunteered. Not the same thing," she assured him with a smile. "Besides, it's only for a couple of days, right? It'll give me more time to concentrate on your house and the different ways I can make it pop."

He had the distinct impression that she already could achieve that result, and not just with his house, but he said nothing and just nodded his head. It was, in the final analysis, a whole lot safer that way.

Chapter Twelve

The thing about Southern California rain was, when it actually did rain, it usually poured.

Kennon rushed the girls from the car into their house. The cloudburst had hit less than ten minutes ago with a fierceness that she'd seldom seen.

Like most Californians, when she heard the weatherman predicting rain at this time of year, she listened with only half an ear.

Rain had its time and place in Southern California, occupying a spate of time referred to as "the rainy season." It stretched from November to March. This, however, being summer, did not fall into that time frame. Consequently, forecasts involving various degrees of precipitation were generally ignored because, like the monsters that lived beneath a young child's bed, they rarely, if ever, actually materialized.

Chalk one up for the weatherman. Even though she

and the girls had dashed all of about ten feet from car door to house door, all three of them were pretty well drenched.

It was a card-carrying storm, all right, Kennon thought, pushing her wet hair out of her eyes.

"You girls stay here," Kennon instructed. She slipped out of her wet shoes, not wanting to leave a trail of puddles to mark her path. Her wet jacket suffered the same fate, hitting the tile beside her shoes. "I'll get you towels and some dry clothes," she promised.

Barefoot, Kennon ran up the stairs quickly, hurrying into their bedrooms to collect the items she'd just mentioned. She was back in less than two minutes, handing out towels and placing dry clothes on the stairs for the girls to pick up and change into.

Madelyn and Meghan lost no time in stripping off their wet clothing and putting on the shirts and jeans that she'd brought down. Dressed and feeling a little better, they took the towels and began rubbing the moisture from their hair.

In Meghan's case, Kennon offered to help. Meghan beamed at her, tilting her head toward her for easier access.

It was an extremely maternal rooted moment.

Someday...

"What about you?" Meghan asked, twisting around so that she could get a better look at her father's friend.

Kennon waved away the little girl's concern. "I'm fine," she assured her easily.

Madelyn frowned. "No, you're not," she protested. "You're all wet." It was an observation filled with compassion. "Don't you want to put on some dry clothes, too?"

She really did, but there was a basic problem with that. "I don't have any dry clothes I can change into here."

Madelyn quickly pointed out, "Dad's got clothes. He wouldn't mind you putting them on," the girl vouched, sliding the towel from her hair.

Kennon didn't know about that. She doubted the man would be thrilled to come home and find her wearing something of his. "Your dad's clothes are too big for me."

Madelyn wouldn't be put off. "He's got sweatpants and a sweatshirt. You can wear those," she said stubbornly. "Dad told me they were supposed to be bigger."

"Yeah," Meghan chimed in. "On purpose." Not to be outdone by her sister, the younger of the Sheffield girls volunteered, "I'll go get them for you!" just before she dashed out of the room.

"No, really, I didn't get that wet," Kennon protested.

Futilely, it turned out, because Meghan was back with her booty almost immediately, the arms of her father's dark blue sweatshirt dragging behind her on the tiled floor.

"Here!" Meghan declared triumphantly, thrusting the sweat clothes at her.

Kennon really didn't think it was a good idea to wear Simon's clothes. There was just something far too intimate about that.

"That's all right, Meghan. I don't need to change," she told her pint-size benefactress, making another attempt to beg off.

The next moment, she felt Madelyn tugging on the bottom of her skirt, wringing out the corner. Several drops fell to the floor. Kennon had a sneaking suspicion that Simon's daughters were as tenacious as pit bulls when it came to getting their way. Stubborn to the nth degree.

She could relate to that, and they were trying to do a good deed. So, for now, Kennon gave in. She'd have plenty of time to change back into her own clothes before Simon came home.

"Point taken," Kennon quipped. "Okay, I'll be right back."

Carrying the sweat suit into the master bathroom upstairs, she had just finished stripping off her clothes and climbing into the sweats when she heard the loud, ominous crack of thunder.

The next second, the overhead bathroom light went out. Less than a minute later, the door burst open.

Meghan, wide-eyed and frightened, barreled into the newly redecorated room.

Kennon scooped the six-year-old into her arms and held the little girl close. Meghan was trembling.

"It's just a storm, honey," she said soothingly, stroking the girl's silky hair.

"The lights are gone. Everything's dark and quiet," she cried, frightened.

"Where's...?"

Kennon didn't get a chance to finish her question, but she didn't need to. Walking out of the bathroom, she saw the subject of her aborted inquiry shifting nervously from foot to foot in the hall right outside the bathroom door.

Madelyn was doing her best not to look as frightened as her sister, but it was easy to see that she was.

"The 'lectricity's gone," the little girl told her, clearly agitated.

"It'll be back soon," Kennon promised. She walked downstairs again and to the living room, still holding Meghan. Madelyn trailed behind her, closer than a shadow.

Madelyn looked around uncertainly. The storm had stolen away the sun and everything appeared oppressively dark and gloomy. "You sure?"

"Very sure. It's always come back before," Kennon added. She set Meghan gently back down on the floor. "I tell you what, why don't we have a campout?"

Madelyn's delicate eyebrows scrunched together over her nose in confusion. "But it's raining outside," she protested.

"A *pretend* campout," Kennon amended. "C'mon," she beckoned.

She led the way to the kitchen. Because of its orientation, the kitchen normally required artificial light by three o'clock. The storm had forced the entire room to be thrown into semidarkness, although there was still just enough light available to make out general shapes.

She would have to fish her flashlight out of her purse, Kennon told herself. Otherwise, the next time she came into the kitchen, she'd have to resort to the Braille system.

Moving quickly about the room, Kennon gathered up all the food and beverages that she could. When it got to be too much for her to hold, she pulled out the bottom of the sweatshirt, forming a kind of catchall apron. She deposited the soda cans and food into it.

Kennon was more than aware that she had two very persistent short people following her every move.

Knowing that they were both too frightened to remain alone in the living room, she wasn't about to send either one of them back to wait for her. Instead, she decided to make them feel useful by putting them to work. She handed each of the sisters some utensils and paper plates to carry back with them.

When she was finished collecting items, she did a quick survey to make sure she hadn't forgotten anything. Just as she finished her inventory, there was another crash of thunder. Both girls jumped, then huddled closer to her. She felt like a mother hen protectively gathering her chicks to her.

"Okay, I think that's everything. Back to the living room, ladies," she instructed. She led the way by only a fraction of an inch. Each girl was all but hermetically sealed either to her left or her right side.

Just before they reached the living room, there was yet another loud crack of thunder. This time it came just on the heels of the flash of lightning. Meghan stopping dead, her eyes open so wide they looked as if they could actually fall out. Game or not, she seemed on the verge of crying.

"That's just the angels bowling," Kennon told her. It was an old legend that she remembered her father telling her when she was about Meghan's age. Back then she was afraid of the loud noise coming from what she'd taken to be God's domain. The idea of angels playing a loud game had helped dissipate her fears.

"Angels bowl?" Madelyn asked, mystified.

"They absolutely do," Kennon answered solemnly. "Angels have hobbies, too, just like we do."

Meghan looked at her, confused. "What's bowling?" she asked.

Crossing to the coffee table and depositing her loot, Kennon laughed. It hadn't occurred to her that the girls might not know what she was referring to. Bowling wasn't exactly all that common in this day and age of video games.

"I'll have to show you sometime," she promised.

Meghan seemed somewhat placated. "Okay." Surveying the loot on the table, she brightened. "Are we going to eat this stuff?" she asked hopefully.

"You bet. And you're both going to help me cook it."

The girls looked at her as if she was about to pull off a magic trick.

The electricity went out at the hospital right in the middle of the surgery he was performing. Thank God for the emergency generator, Simon thought. It kicked in almost immediately, allowing him to complete the surgery.

Still, the diminished power gave the procedure an eeriness he wasn't comfortable with.

"Power's out all over Newport Beach and Bedford," one of the surgical nurses complained to an orderly as the latter wheeled the patient toward the double-doored recovery room.

Simon thought of his daughters. Both Meghan and Madelyn slept with night-lights on because they were afraid of the dark. Madelyn had outgrown her fears, but had regressed after her mother died. The girls had to be scared to death.

The moment he felt that his patient was stable and recovering well from the bypass surgery, despite the unfortunate glitch in power, Simon quickly changed out of his scrubs. Five minutes later, he was hurrying into the parking structure to retrieve his car.

The trip back to his development turned out to be an ordeal. Since he was in a hurry, he found his patience strained to the limit. With the power failure still very much in effect, every single traffic light had gone out and the principle of stop signs had to be invoked in order to prevent a slew of accidents from taking place. That meant incredible tie-ups. It also meant stopping at each intersection leading up to the freeway.

He found the same situation in effect when he got off the freeway. Consequently, the trip home took more than three times as long as it ordinarily did.

By the time he reached his house, he felt as if he could literally snap off the steering wheel with his bare hands.

His concern for his daughters all but overwhelmed him.

Simon dropped his house key twice trying to get it into the lock. Biting off a curse, he finally succeeded. He threw open the door, was about to race in, calling out to his daughters, when he heard something that stopped him dead in his tracks.

It took a moment for the sound to register properly in his head.

Singing.

No, he hadn't imagined it. He heard voices raised in song, singing what sounded like—

"Twenty-seven bottles of soda on the wall?" he questioned, confused as he took in the scene.

Kennon and the girls were sitting on a blanket in front of the fireplace. The latter was the only source of illumination in the room, thanks to the fire that had been lit.

Obviously the logs were not just for show.

The moment they heard him, the singing stopped. Madelyn and Meghan scrambled up to their feet and launched themselves at their father, forming a tangle of arms and legs, embraces and kisses. They all but brought him down to the floor in their enthusiasm.

"Daddy, you made it!" Meghan cried happily. "You came home!"

"I told Meggie you would," Madelyn informed him in the best grown-up voice she could manage. He noticed, though, that his older daughter sniffled slightly as she said it.

His arms around both girls, Simon looked over toward the woman rising to her feet in the background. Remnants of what had to have been a meal were on the blanket she had spread out on the rug before the hearth. The warmth of the scene got to him before he fully realized it.

"I guess I shouldn't have bothered worrying," he said, relieved and oddly stirred at the same time.

His eyes narrowed a little. What was the woman wearing?

"The girls came through like troupers," Kennon informed him proudly.

That was only because she was here, he thought. He doubted that even Edna would have been able to keep them not just calm, but from the looks of it, happily engaged while thunder roared overhead.

"How did you get them to forget about the storm?" he asked.

"I know a lot of Girl Scout songs," she quipped with

an infectious grin. "We've been singing—and eating—
for a while now."

She saw the curious way Simon looked at her. And
then she realized why. He was probably wondering about
the sweat suit she was wearing.

How could she have forgotten to change back into
her own clothes? She'd known he'd be back. The trouble
was, she'd gotten caught up in entertaining Madelyn and
Meghan. Changing had completely slipped her mind.

"Can we camp out, Daddy?" Meghan piped up, her
small face lit up with hope.

She was kidding, right? "Honey, it's kind of wet outside," Simon tactfully pointed out.

"No." Meghan shook her head. "I mean in here. Can
we camp out in here?"

Madelyn added her voice to the verbal assault. "Kennon said we had to ask you, but if you say yes, she said
she can put up sheets to make the tents and stuff. Please,
Daddy?" his daughter begged.

"Yeah, please, Daddy?" Meghan echoed, tugging on
the bottom of his jacket to add emphasis to her pleas.
"Say yes."

The days of childhood long behind him, he had a
very limited imagination. It wouldn't have occurred to
him to set up a pseudo-camp in the living room, or to
use bedsheets in place of the real thing. He had to hand
it to the woman, Kennon was creative.

Not to mention subtly gorgeous in that oversize sweat
suit—which, if he wasn't mistaken, looked *extremely*
familiar.

"Sure. I wouldn't want to be the one to rain on your
parade," he said.

Kennon winced at his choice of words. "No pun intended, right?"

Simon inclined his head. "Well, maybe just a little," he admitted. "So, how do we pitch these things?" he asked, setting Meghan down on the floor again.

He had to be tired after putting in a full day. She didn't want to impose on him any more than she really needed to. "You tell me which sheets we can use and leave the rest to me."

He liked the way she took charge, liked the independence that she displayed. Both were traits he'd always admired in people.

"I'll do better than that. I'll go get them for you," he volunteered.

The next moment, he went up the stairs to fetch a couple of old sets from the bottom of the linen closet. Sheets that Edna had told him she was storing "just in case." The nanny never went into any detail as to what ramifications she was applying to "just in case," but he had a feeling that this would definitely meet with the woman's approval.

As Kennon already had.

Studying her for the next hour or so, Simon began to wonder if there was any challenge out there that Kennon wasn't up to. She had not only managed to tame the girls' fears, but had made them cheerful about the ordeal and even hopeful that the storm would last "a little longer so we can camp out like this tomorrow night, too."

He had a sneaking suspicion that what they especially liked was the fact that they got notes from him, per Kennon's request, to their teachers, explaining why they couldn't bring in their homework. It was more or less a given, actually. Assignments were sent home via email on the computers and since there was no power, there was no email.

He marveled at how well she rose to the occasion. Rather than resort to something at room temperature, Kennon had made them a regular dinner. Taking the pork loin she'd found in the refrigerator, she'd fashioned a spit and roasted the meat in the fireplace.

"This is the way it was done when the pioneers made their way west to California," she told the girls, who watched her every move with awe.

Eating as if they'd been starving for days, both girls absorbed everything Kennon told them as if it was gospel.

"Were you a piney-ear?" Meghan asked as she finished the last of her second helping.

"Pioneer," Madelyn corrected her with a sniff and a toss of her head. She smiled proudly that she had gotten the word right.

"No, I wasn't," Kennon answered, noting that Simon struggled not to laugh. "But I did read about them when I was around your age." History had always fascinated her, even before it was a required subject in school.

"Can we read about them, too?" Meghan asked, eager to emulate her.

"You sure can," Kennon replied. "I think I still have some of those books in my library at home." She saw the curious expression on Simon's face. "My dad used to give me history books for Christmas and my birthday." She knew that probably sounded strange to him. "My father said he wanted me to use my mind."

Simon nodded his approval. He was still trying to

find just the right balance as a father. Anyone who made it earned his admiration. "Sounds like a smart man."

"He was." Even as she said it, Kennon sighed, wishing that her father had been more accessible to her. She never got the chance to try to bridge the gap. He'd died shortly after her parents had divorced.

Simon glanced at his watch. It was later than he'd thought. "Time for bed, girls."

For once, the girls were too tired to argue. Besides, *bed* didn't mean bed, it meant the tent, and they were eager to spend the night inside the structure that Kennon had put up for them. Changing into their pajamas, they were ready for bed in record time.

Ten minutes into the story that they begged Kennon to tell them, both little girls were sound asleep.

"Maybe I should try shutting off the power myself once in a while," Simon commented.

Suddenly fidgety inside, Kennon gathered up the dirty dishes from the blanket before the fireplace and took them into the kitchen.

Simon followed her. "Why don't you leave those for now?"

It went against her principles, but this was his house, not hers, so she nodded. "All right."

Dusting off her hands, she walked back into the living room. The rain began to come down harder, pounding down on the roof.

"I guess I'd better be going," she said, looking around for her purse.

As if to argue with her, another rumble of thunder came less than five seconds after a bright flash of lightning had creased the sky, momentarily lighting up the world.

He didn't want her out on the road in this weather. "Maybe you better stay until it lets up a little," Simon suggested quietly.

Kennon paused for a moment, wondering if perhaps she was safer out in the storm than in here.

A warmth surrounded her when she thought of staying here with Simon under these conditions. If she had an iota of common sense, she'd leave.

Temptation won out.

"Maybe," Kennon allowed, wavering, "just for a little bit."

Because she couldn't just stand there in the middle of the room, looking into his incredibly blue eyes, she crossed over to the sofa.

Like someone trying to pull herself out of a trance, Kennon lowered herself onto the sofa, acutely aware that her lungs felt more than a wee bit short of breath.

And she knew why.

Chapter Thirteen

For a long moment, the only sound heard was the crackle of the fire and the insistent tapping of the rain against the windows.

And then Simon spoke. "By the way, I have to ask." His eyes indicated the sweat suit she wore. "Is that mine?"

Embarrassment whispered along her cheeks, shading them all over again. Why hadn't she remembered to change back? Or, better yet, why hadn't she said no to the girls in the first place?

"Yes," she murmured, then added, "I'm sorry."

He didn't quite follow her. "For what?"

She started to explain, aware that the bottom line was that she was the adult and should have been the one to draw the line, not give in to two girls under the age of nine.

"After I had the girls change out of their wet clothes,

they insisted I do the same." She shrugged. "I told them that I didn't have any extra clothes with me, which was when Meghan ran into your room and grabbed these." She looked down at the sweatshirt she had slipped on. "They forced me to get out of my clothes and put yours on."

"I would like to have seen that." And then, seeing the intriguing shade of deep pink that came over her cheeks, he realized what Kennon thought he was saying, and quickly clarified. "Having two pint-size little women force you to do what they said. I didn't mean to imply—"

She threw up her hand, as if to physically stop his words.

"I know you didn't," she said quickly, sparing them both the embarrassment of having what they were thinking put into words.

"You said that awfully quickly," Simon observed. He had no idea why he was suddenly playing devil's advocate, or why he was so intrigued with her blush, but wondering didn't deter him. "Are you that sure that I wouldn't have those kinds of thoughts? I'm not a robot, Kennon, even though at times I might seem as if I'm on automatic pilot."

She hadn't meant to insult him.

Kennon let out a long, ragged breath, trying to pull herself together. The way Simon watched her flustered her and made her feel insanely warm all over. Far warmer than anything the fire in the hearth could achieve on its own.

"I don't think of you as a robot," she heard herself saying. Her mouth incredibly bone-dry, each word she uttered felt as if she was measuring it out slowly. Almost *too* slowly.

She'd managed to stir his curiosity. "Oh? How do you think of me?"

She went blank. Her brain felt like a field mouse, lost in a darkened warehouse, searching for the path home. Desperate, she said the first thing that came to her. "As the girls' father."

He was that, but suddenly, without examining why, he wanted more. "And that's all?"

Kennon could feel her heart pound erratically, as if any second now, it would break out of her chest.

"No," she admitted, her voice barely above a whisper, "that's not all."

Sitting next to her, Simon read between the lines. "Am I making you uncomfortable, Kennon?"

Now, there was an understatement, she thought.

"Yes." Realizing what she'd just said and how it had to sound to him, she amended her response. "No." But Kennon knew that that wasn't strictly true, so she settled for "Maybe," accompanying the word with a vague, half shrug.

"Well, that about covers it all, doesn't it?" he said, amused. "Yes, no and maybe." He paused for a second, smiled, and then said, "Ditto."

It was Kennon's turn to be confused. She shook her head. "Excuse me?"

"Ditto," Simon obligingly repeated for her. "That means—"

She stopped him before he could get further sidetracked. "I know what the word means." That wasn't what she was asking. "But why would I make you uncomfortable?"

If he were someone else, a flippant answer would come to his lips, shielding him. But he wasn't someone else and any answer he gave had to be the truth.

"Because you're making me feel things, Kennon, things I was certain I would never be able to feel again. And it's uncomfortable because it hurts to feel again. Hurts and yet it's…" He searched for a word to describe this new/old territory he found himself wandering through. The only one that came to mind was "exhilarating."

He cupped her cheek, his eyes on hers, knowing that he was treading on dangerous ground. The ice was thin beneath his feet and any second, liable to crack, sending him plummeting into the freezing water. He crossed anyway.

"Part of me doesn't want 'this' and part of me is so relieved to be back among the living again." He stopped and shook his head. To his own ear, he sounded as if he was just babbling. "Is any of this making any sense to you at all?"

Kennon pressed her lips together. "Yes. An infinite amount of sense," she finally told him haltingly. "And I do understand."

Because she was afraid, too.

Afraid to care, afraid of being hurt. She hadn't suffered through a spouse's death, but she'd experienced the death of love, the death of something she thought she had, but didn't, and that carried its own pain with it. And its own unique set of fears.

"Then I'm not losing my mind?" he asked with a self-deprecating laugh.

Instead of answering him verbally, Kennon leaned over and kissed him.

It was meant to be a soft, reassuring kiss, a silent affirmation that she was experiencing the same kind of confusing feelings that he was.

Passion wasn't supposed to be part of the equation, but it was there suddenly, uninvited and taking control of the situation like a well-trained commando. Opening doors that had been shut, making sensations suddenly burst loose of their shackles. It swiftly and completely filled the emptiness with its presence, like a plastic life raft being set free.

The pulse that had been hammering inside her with increased urgency suddenly went into triple time. *This* was what they had to be talking about when they said "instant chemistry," because she felt it, felt the attraction, full-blown and overwhelming, that had seized her the moment she had pressed her lips to his.

Her head swirled as she lost her bearings as well as herself in the kiss that he deepened. Deepened to the point that it became bottomless—and she was spiraling down into it.

Oh, no, he shouldn't be doing this.

Granted, Kennon had technically started it, but he was supposed to be strong enough to just pull away, not leap into the center of it like a starving man leaped into a banquet.

But there was no denying that she didn't *just* stir him—he could walk away from that if it involved sex, even though admittedly it would be difficult—she made him feel as if she'd set him on fire.

She made him want her with a fierceness that went down to his very bones. Made him aware that he had needs he would have *sworn* no longer existed. Needs that now urgently *begged* to be addressed and sated.

The kiss grew in length and depth and strength, engulfing him as well as her. Collectively taking them prisoner. He didn't feel he was in control of what was going on and suspected that neither did she. This was bigger than either one of them.

His breath was stolen away, along with his will, and while a small part of him still clung to the belief that, at the end, he could break away, for now Simon allowed himself to be swept away. He savored and absorbed what had been gone from his life for so many long, haunting months.

His lips left hers, moving to other parts of her face and neck, raining a multitude of kisses on each new place he found.

The kisses multiplied in number and strength, even as he struggled to contain his hunger and the growing desire within him that threatened to consume him if left unfulfilled.

Lost in a burning haze, Simon still felt her hands on his chest, felt Kennon pushing him back, at first so lightly he thought he was imagining it, and then with more force.

She'd changed her mind, he thought.

At least one of them had the strength to stop this before there was no turning back.

A sense of loss pervaded through him.

But before he could say anything, before he could acknowledge that he hadn't meant for things to get out of hand this way, Kennon breathlessly said, "The girls," and without further elaboration, he knew what she meant, what she was trying to tell him.

They couldn't do this in front of his daughters, even if the girls were both sound asleep.

"You want to stop."

Kennon took it as a question. And as such, answered it, correcting him. "I want to go upstairs."

He wasn't prepared for the excitement that pulsated through him in response to her words. Even so, he stifled the very real urge to sweep her into his arms and carry her off to his room without another word, fearing that word might represent a change of heart on her part.

But Simon knew he couldn't live with himself if he took advantage of their mutual insanity without giving Kennon a chance to think things through. And in doing so, to change her mind.

So he looked into her eyes and asked her, "Are you sure?"

For now, she had managed to banish Pete's memory and the damage it had done to her heart and to her self-esteem. She'd eradicated everything from her mind but this moment and this man. And the way he made her feel: glorious and immortal.

"I'm sure," she whispered, surprised that she could actually form words and speak.

Simon glanced back over his shoulder toward where his daughters were sleeping. He wanted to assure himself that they were really asleep.

One peek into the tent gave him his answer.

Barring the earth opening up beneath them, his daughters appeared in deep slumber.

Wordlessly, he linked the fingers of his right hand with Kennon's left and led the way upstairs. The moment they were in his room, he closed the door behind him.

Turning toward the woman who had raised his body

temperature to really dangerous levels, he said, "Last chance."

Her eyes on his, Kennon raised herself up on her toes. She threaded her arms around his neck. "No, I hope not," she murmured just before she pressed her lips to his.

And reignited them both.

A mutual frenzy instantly seized them, as if they were both acutely aware that they were on borrowed time and had to make the most of the minutes they had.

His mouth now sealed to hers, Simon tugged on the sweatshirt, pulling it up along her torso and then off her arms. He sent it to the floor a beat before he began to do the same to her sweatpants. In almost slow motion, he moved the soft material down the length of her legs. Exciting her.

Exciting himself.

When the sweatpants pooled about her ankles, Kennon gingerly stepped out of them.

That was when he realized that all she had left on was a thong.

His throat threatened to close on him.

Simon felt her lips draw back into a smile beneath his. "I guess you want your sweat suit back," she murmured, her words fading into his mouth.

The thought of her scent imprinted on his sweat clothes sent his senses scrambling with deep anticipation. As did the feel of her hands on his body as she began to slowly peel away his clothes from his skin.

Impatience seized him a moment later and it became a joint effort.

The feel of her long fingers along his bare skin enflamed Simon, making him want more.

Their clothes in a jumbled heap on the floor, he pressed her down onto his bed. Struggling to hold himself in check a few moments longer, Simon shifted his weight away from her.

Just as she was about to ask if anything was wrong, he began pleasuring her with his hands, with his teeth and then his lips as he reveled in the feel, the scent, the very taste of her.

The more he did, the more he wanted her until he thought he would explode or dissolve if he didn't seal their union.

Shifting Kennon so that she was beneath him again, Simon slowly slid his body along over hers. He locked his hands with hers and became part of her as the ultimate moment beckoned to him.

His hips rocked against hers with more and more intensity until, locked in a kiss, he felt rather than heard her cry out his name. At the same time, he felt her name echo in his throat.

The starburst receded.

The ensuing euphoria gentled until it faded away into a whisper.

As it faded, guilt beckoned to him, growing more and more urgent in its demands and he struggled to keep it at bay.

What could he say to her, Simon wondered as their breathing began to settle into a regular pattern. *Thank you? I'm sorry?* Neither response seemed right or even remotely adequate.

He hadn't meant to do this, even though he'd wanted to with every fiber of his being.

"Kennon," he finally began, his voice all but hoarse. "I—"

She could hear it. Hear the regret. The apology. She didn't want to hear it, not yet, not while she was hugging the moment, the sensations that had given her life.

Rather than let Simon utter another word, she turned in to him and then shifted so that she was on top of him, straddling his body with her own. Silencing the words with her mouth on his.

The blood still surging wildly in her veins, Kennon began to make love *to* him all over again, nipping at his lips, pressing kisses along his neck and chest, running her fingertips lightly along his hard body, until she'd managed to bring him around, arousing Simon and getting him to join in the venture. And then, just like that, she was making love *with* him the way she wanted, not just *to* him.

The wildness that had seized them both the first time around now settled into a more temperate pace, allowing them to savor rather than devour, to roam rather than speed. And to enjoy this revisit the way they hadn't allowed themselves to enjoy the journey originally.

Time stood still as they made love languidly.

And somewhere along the line, while all this was going on, though she did it against her will and most definitely without her consent, Kennon lost her heart to him.

Completely.

Chapter Fourteen

The thunder had stopped. The rain continued, tapping on the roof in a steady rhythm. The house remained bathed in darkness as somewhere outside, slicker-clothed crews from the electric company valiantly struggled to restore power to the downed areas.

Simon had no idea what time it was, only that it was night and that for the first time in many months, he was not alone in his bed.

The perfume that Kennon wore subtly drifted into his consciousness. He held her in his arms, waiting for the beating of his heart to settle. Waiting for order to be restored to his body. To his world.

Eventually, the short, heavy breathing became longer, easier. He banished all thoughts from his mind, struggling to enjoy this moment in time for as long as he could.

Kennon lay beside him, curled against his body,

listening to Simon breathe. Listening until his even breathing told her that he was asleep. It took a long while, but she was finally satisfied.

Afraid of the conversation once he woke up, afraid of detecting regret in his eyes and most afraid that Simon would see something altogether different in hers when he looked, Kennon slowly slipped out of his bed.

Picking up the discarded sweat suit, she laid it across a chair, then quickly went into the bathroom, where she'd left the wet clothing she'd stripped off hours ago.

A lifetime ago.

The clothes were still damp, but that didn't really matter to her. It was an inconvenience, not a problem.

What mattered right now was making good her escape before Simon opened his eyes again and shattered this lovely interlude she was holding close to her heart.

She was behaving like a coward, a role that was not just foreign to her, but odious, as well. But right now, she just couldn't face reality. This way, if she left before Simon woke up, she would be able to cling to the sensation that making love with him, not once, but three times, three *glorious* times, created within her.

There would be plenty of time down the line to come to her senses, to place tonight on the shelf with the other broken dreams that littered her life. For now she just wanted to go on being happy, and she knew that she could only do that if she continued to maintain this world of illusions that was swirling around her.

Using her fingers to comb back her hair, Kennon deliberately avoided looking at herself in the mirror. With her shoes pressed to her chest, rather than on her feet, where she would risk making noise and waking him up, Kennon sneaked out of first the bathroom and then his bedroom.

Once outside Simon's door, she eased it closed again and made her way down the stairs.

Mercifully, the dying light from the fireplace illuminated the living room, so the search for her purse went quickly enough. The sound of harmonious, even breathing told her that the girls were still asleep.

There was no one to impede her getaway.

She had no idea why that thought saddened her, when making a quick, soundless escape was all she told herself she wanted. But a sadness did descend over her, taking her prisoner and making it hard for her to even breathe.

The oppressive sadness all but flattened her as she stepped outside. Kennon closed the front door behind her in slow motion, the tempo created by an overwhelming reluctance to leave.

Snapping out of it, she forced herself to make her way quickly to her car. She hardly noticed—and cared less—that the rain was beating down on her.

Kennon was completely drenched by the time she reached her vehicle and got inside. It made no difference one way or another. She was too busy struggling to keep her tears from falling to care about the small puddle forming on the floor mat beneath the pedals.

No doubt about it. She'd failed miserably at hanging on to the euphoria that had been so strong just a few minutes earlier.

Putting her key in the ignition, she started the car and immediately backed out of Simon's driveway. Flooring the accelerator, she drove away quickly before she could change her mind and go back.

As the rain beat down on her windshield, Kennon gave up trying not to cry.

* * *

The shifting bed had roused him from what had been a light sleep at best. Before he could open his eyes, Kennon had slipped out of his bed. Simon assumed that she was just visiting the bathroom.

He pretended to still be asleep. The ruse bought him a little time. His mind raced about, searching for something to say to her in the aftermath of their lovemaking.

Something that didn't express regret, or hint at the fact that he was silently battling a surge of guilt. Surprisingly enough, it wasn't as big a surge as he'd anticipated.

He'd honestly expected to drown in the emotion. Since his wife had been killed, he hadn't so much as taken a woman out to dinner, much less completely lost himself in her to the point of making love with sheer abandonment.

But that was what had happened tonight. He'd completely lost himself in Kennon, not just in the act of lovemaking, but in the act of making love *with* her and *to* her. What had happened here wasn't just about a body, or a face, or about an unaddressed urge that had demanded attention.

This involved a great deal more.

Kennon actually *mattered* to him.

The fact that she did surprised him, as well. He hadn't thought himself capable of having feelings, much less feelings so strong that they delved down to his bones. Feelings that demanded he act on them or wind up disintegrating right where he stood.

Simon didn't know how to handle that. He didn't know what Kennon would expect him to say once they were facing each other and the passion had cooled down enough to be manageable.

So he lay there in the dark, listening to the rain and straining to hear the sound of her returning to his bed. And trying to think of something to say that would entangle neither one of them until he could decide what this actually meant to him.

When the bathroom door had opened and he'd narrowed his eyes to tiny slits, still pretending to be asleep, Simon had been surprised to realize that she was intent on slipping out of the room without waking him.

She wasn't just stepping into the bathroom to respond to a call of nature, she'd gone in to put her clothes back on.

She was leaving, otherwise she would have put the sweat suit back on.

That bought him more time to sort things out. What it didn't bring him was a sense of peace.

Even though he was somewhat relieved, he couldn't help wondering why she was leaving. Why, after the time they'd spent together, after the way their souls had all but touched, did she suddenly feel so compelled to leave his bed and his house without a word?

It didn't make sense to him.

Neither did his quick surrender to the demands that his attraction to her had evoked. But there was no denying that both had happened.

Simon sat up. For a split second, he thought of going after her, of bringing Kennon back before she could walk out the door. But if he did that, then he'd have to say something to her and he had absolutely no idea what that would be.

His brain was numb.

"I had a great time, thanks" was inane and didn't even begin to cover it. But any sentiment beyond that might make Kennon think that they were on the road to "something" and he honestly didn't know if they were. He might not be able to deal with the guilt—and the dire, underlying fear of possible loss. He had no idea if he was strong enough for that.

Simon scrubbed his hand over his face. He'd never felt so confused before, never felt so many emotions running through him at the same time as he did right at this moment.

With a sigh, he fell back on the bed. Who said that getting through adolescence was the hardest part? Adolescence had been a cakewalk compared to this.

And it felt as if things would only get harder.

So he didn't get up, he didn't get dressed and he didn't go running after her. Instead, he remained where he was, willing himself to fall back asleep and let oblivion take over.

It was a long time before he got his wish.

As he unlocked the front door to the shop, Nathan appeared perplexed not to hear an annoying, high-pitched noise. That was the warning signal that he had forty-five seconds to disarm the security system before it began making more noise than a puppy dashing through a bell factory.

Nathan stopped, listening. Soon he turned around and stifled a cry. He grabbed his chest to keep his heart from leaping out of his shallow rib cage.

A ragged sigh broke free as he struggled to calm down.

"Damn it, Kennon, you scared me half to death,"

he declared, not bothering to block out the annoyance from his voice. Taking another deep breath, he dropped his hand to his side and crossed over to Kennon, who was seated at her drawing board. "What are you doing here?"

"I work here, remember?" she said glibly. Although, if she didn't come up with something soon, she wouldn't hold on to this place much longer, she thought, frustrated as she stared down at the blank page.

"No, you don't," Nathan contradicted, drawing closer. When she looked at him sharply, he said, "The woman who works here hasn't been around for almost a month, except to pop her head in a couple of times before dashing off again."

Her eyes narrowed. She wasn't in the mood for his repartee. "And to give you your paycheck."

"Well, yes," Nathan conceded with a quick shrug of one shoulder, "there's that, too. But then, you had to, didn't you? I'm carrying the weight here lately and last I'd heard, the slaves had been freed by that nice, tall guy in the beard and stovepipe hat." Nathan pretended to scrutinize her as he slowly looked her up and down. "I'd like to see some ID, please."

She let out an annoyed sigh. "You can be replaced, you know."

He responded by nodding with satisfaction. "Now, that's the Kennon we all know and love." He glanced at the empty pad and frowned slightly to himself. Rather than comment on it, he asked, "So what are you doing back—besides slumming?"

As he spoke, Nathan shed his fashionable black trench coat.

"And while we're at it," he said, circling her slowly

and appraising Kennon from all possible angles, "any particular reason you look like something the cat would be embarrassed dragging in?" In front of her again, he raised a quizzical eyebrow. "Trouble in paradise?"

She really didn't need flippant today. She just wanted to bury herself in her work. There were still things she had to finish up doing at Simon's house before she could move on.

As no doubt he would, too, she thought.

The sun had been up a full three hours and so, undoubtedly, had he and the girls. The phone hadn't rung once. Not her landline—she'd put it on call forwarding—or her cell. If he cared, he would have called. But he hadn't, ergo, he didn't. She was a big girl, she understood that what had happened last night didn't immediately lead to "happily-ever-after."

Or, in her case, ever.

"There *is* no paradise," she said shortly.

"That's a matter of opinion." Taking off his jacket, Nathan began to carefully roll up his sleeves, folding over the material on first one, then the other. "I've seen the way Doctor Hunk looks at you—and the way you look at him. Moreover, when you *have* been in, I've had to suffer through listening to you hum—very badly off-key, I might add. If *that* doesn't have paradise written all over it, then I'm a wooden boy with strings whose nose grows." The moment Nathan made the pronouncement, he looked at her more closely. A touch of sympathy entered his voice. "There *is* trouble in paradise, isn't there?"

"Stop calling it that," Kennon warned him, danger-ously close to snapping. "Dr. Simon Sheffield is just another client."

"Uh-huh, and the Olympics are just another bunch of games." Nathan perched himself on the edge of her desk, careful not to tilt the board. "Talk to me, Kennon," he instructed. "What happened?"

"Nothing happened," she insisted.

This was a mistake, coming in today, she thought as despair seeped into her. But she hadn't wanted to stay home, either, alone with her thoughts, examining last night from every angle and regretting it. Work was not just her passion, but her therapy, as well. It defined who and what she was, and there were times, like when Pete had dumped her, that it stitched together her body and soul. But if she was going to be subjected to Nathan's interrogation, then she just wouldn't come around. She might as well be home, eating a half gallon of mint-chip ice cream and playing that CD with the collection of songs she'd picked up several years ago, the one that lamented the stupidity of falling in love in the first place.

Kennon abruptly stood up. Nathan followed suit, reading her mind and blocking her escape.

His fingers were long and bony but surprisingly strong as he clamped his hands down on her shoulders to hold her in place.

"Something most definitely *did* happen and you have to tell me what," he informed her. When she said nothing, he tried logic. "You know you have to get it out in the open." When she still said nothing and then shrugged him off, Nathan played his ace. "Don't make me bring out the big guns," he warned. Reaching into his pocket, he pulled out his cell phone and held it up for her to see. "I have your mother on speed dial and I'm not afraid to press the button."

Kennon closed her eyes and sighed. Oh, God, not her mother. Not now. She just wasn't up to having the woman descend on her. She wasn't up to the questions she knew her mother would fire at her like a discharging AK-47. She wasn't up to the sympathy, along with pity, her mother would display and she *definitely* was not up to hearing the barrage of suggestions that would come at her from every direction.

Ruth Cassidy was one of those people who truly believed she could fix anything she set her mind to—no matter how long it took. Kennon did *not* want to be this month's project.

Taking a deep breath, Kennon went with the lesser of two evils. She told Nathan what he wanted to hear. "I slept with him."

Nathan waited for more. It didn't come and he frowned. "Forgive me, but isn't that a good thing?"

You'd think that, wouldn't you? After all, she hadn't so much as held hands with a man since the Pete fiasco. "Not in this case."

"Oh. I see." Each word Nathan uttered had an inordinate amount of time between it and the next one. He nodded to underscore the fact that he understood what the problem was. Disappointment. "He's lousy in bed. I'm sorry." Nathan shook his head in sympathy. "And he looked like he had such potential, too." He sighed, able to relate. "Just goes to show that you really *can't* tell a book by its cover."

Oh, God, he would go on like this all morning if she didn't set him straight.

"No, he's not lousy in bed," she told Nathan. The man looked at her, puzzled. "He's—" Kennon searched for a word that would cover the situation without being gushy. This was not a topic she wanted up for discussion. Now or ever. Her back to the wall, she went with the all-purpose word *good*. Then, because Nathan was still watching her expectantly, waiting for more, she added, "Very good."

"Okay," he allowed, "The doctor is good in bed. Very good," he underscored, mimicking her tone. "Then what's the problem?"

She was *not* getting any work done, was she? "The problem is he's in love with his wife."

Nathan's perfectly shaped eyebrows rose high on his forehead. "He's married?" her assistant cried, indignant and horrified for her at the same time. "When did this come out?"

She shook her head. "No, he's not married, he's a widower."

Abject confusion replaced angry indignation. Nathan connected his own set of dots. And then he sighed. "Contrary to the philosophy espoused by some of the currently trendy horror movies, the dead don't come back to haunt the living."

"He's not haunted by her," she told Nathan, really wishing he would drop the subject, knowing at the same time that he wouldn't until he was satisfied with her explanation. "He just feels guilty having feelings about anyone else."

Nathan's frown deepened as he tried to follow the logic. "And Doctor Hunk said this to you after the fact—?"

"No."

"Before the fact? The man issued a disclaimer before you and he tripped the light fantastic?"

Nathan had the strangest frame of reference she'd ever heard. "No, not in so many words—"

Nathan stopped her. "Did he say it to you in *any* words?" he asked.

She closed her eyes and sighed. How could she have forgotten that Nathan was relentless? He'd badgered her like this the last time, until she'd told him all about Pete breaking up with her. And then she'd had to restrain him from making good on his promise of breaking into Pete's house and putting crushed oleanders into his salad dressing because he'd read that oleanders were an odorless, tasteless way to poison someone.

"No, but I just felt it, that's all—"

Nathan held up his hand. "So let me get this straight. You're here, looking like a truck just ran over your favorite puppy, because, after spending a torrid night of wickedly wonderful lovemaking, you're *assuming* Prince Charming is going to say something less than princely?" Nathan shook his head. "Do you know how stupid that sounds?"

"Not until you just said it out loud," Kennon countered.

He inclined his head, satisfied. Now he could get back to work. "Good, then my work here is done." He gestured her toward the front door. "Go back to the man, tell him you were sleepwalking, but you're awake now and in full possession of your senses. Or," he amended glibly, "in as much possession as you can manage."

Kennon stayed where she was. She frowned. "It's not that easy."

"Sure it is," Nathan contradicted. "You're the one who's making it hard." About to get behind Kennon to push her out the door, he stopped when he looked outside the front of the shop. "Speak of the devil."

"What devil?" Kennon turned around to look. The air completely whooshed out of her lungs as the bell announcing a customer's entrance went off.

And Simon walked into the shop.

Chapter Fifteen

The silence stretched out as they stared at one another.

Finally, his face an emotionless mask, Simon said quietly, "You left."

Was he accusing her, or stating a fact with quiet relief? She couldn't tell. Kennon pressed her lips together. They felt as dry as parchment.

"Pick up on that, did you?" she cracked, trying desperately to lighten the tension all but pressing down on her.

His eyes narrowed as he ignored her attempt at humor. "Why did you leave?"

What did she say to that? That she was afraid he'd see how much she loved him if she stayed? That she was afraid he'd push her away? That her fear of rejection made her flee? Was there any way to word this, to tell him the truth, without seeming needy to him?

Kennon was about to try to frame an answer when she realized that they were not alone in the showroom. Nathan stood to her left as if he had every right to be there listening to their exchange. The man might very well be the best friend she had, but right now, Nathan had no business being part of this very personal scenario—not until she figured out her own role in it and was willing to share it with him.

Turning toward Nathan, she asked, "Don't you have something to do in the storeroom?"

If he realized what she was trying to do, he gave her no indication. "No."

It wasn't that Nathan was dense when it came to hints, Kennon thought. He was being stubborn.

"Sure you do," she insisted. When he continued looking at her as if she was wasting her breath, trying to jar his memory or engage his cooperation, she pointedly said, "You have to be in it."

With a dramatic sigh and what appeared to be the beginning of an even more dramatic rolling of his eyes, Nathan turned on his very expensive heel and headed to the back of the store. Walking particularly slowly, he finally disappeared around the corner.

When Simon took that moment to begin to talk to her, Kennon held her hand up. Without looking back at him, she silently asked Simon to hold his peace a moment longer until she was finished.

"The door, Nathan," she called out, raising her voice. "Close the door, please."

A second later, she heard the sound of the storeroom door meeting its frame. The meeting did not occur quietly. Satisfied that Nathan had shut the door behind him as she'd requested, she turned around to face Simon again.

She tried desperately to steel herself, bracing for a verbal mortal blow. "You were saying?"

"No," he corrected tersely, his eyes on hers, "you were." When Kennon remained silent, he prompted, "You were going to tell me why you left not just my bed, but my house in the middle of the night."

Why was he pushing this? They'd made love and, even while they were in the throes of it, they both knew where it was headed. Straight into oblivion. What she'd done was make the awkward small talk unnecessary. And now here he was, digging it up.

"I wanted to make it easy on you," she told him, struggling to keep any emotion out of her voice.

"And how, exactly, was finding you gone after we'd spent half the night making love together making it 'easy' on me?" he asked.

She stared past his head. It was the only way she could keep from letting the tears flow—and from doubling her hands into fists and beating on him.

"I figured I'd spare you having to say something along the lines of, 'It was great, but it was just one of those things,' and not to expect a replay. Or worse, you'd give apologizing to me a shot."

"Apologizing," he echoed. "Why?" Simon asked. "Why would I be apologizing?" He came up with the only answer he could. "Was it that bad for you?"

"No!" she cried.

How could he even *think* that? He'd rocked her whole world, not once, but three times, each better than the last, a feat that was uncanny in itself. She'd never felt that wondrous before, that ready to literally sprout wings and fly up to the heavens so that she might touch the sky.

Because she could see he was waiting for an explanation, she stumbled ahead, searching for words, for a way to make him understand what she didn't fully understand herself. Fear was a paralyzing force.

Kennon picked her way carefully through the minefield. "I was afraid that maybe what happened last night between us was just a matter of time and place and conditions—"

He stared at her, trying to make sense out of what she was saying, and getting nowhere. Finally, he asked, "Do you come with subtitles, because I'm really not following this."

She sighed. If she'd had any sense at all, she wouldn't have let things go as far as they had last night—for as many times as they did. A true survivor would have left at the first hint of a kiss, not hung around, waiting to get her hair curled.

But what was done was done and she had to make the best of it.

"Look, I talked to Edna when I first started working on your house. I know you love your wife—your late wife," Kennon amended, "and I don't want you to feel guilty, or worse, get angry at me for being in the right place at the right time or the wrong place at the wrong time, or however you want to think about what happened between us." She could see that he wasn't following her any better than he had been a moment ago. She tried again. "And if you want to know the truth—"

"Please," he stressed with feeling.

She forced herself to look into Simon's deep blue eyes. "I don't want to be dumped again."

"So you're dumping me in order not to be dumped?"

"Not dumped," she cried. "I wasn't 'dumping' you, I was just...slipping away," she finally said, but even saying that didn't feel right to her. But it *was* what she'd felt, what had motivated her. "Look, last night was wonderful. Maybe almost *too* wonderful," she admitted. "I don't want anything to take away from that. I'd rather just end on a high note and not have it degenerate into something less perfect." She wanted no recriminations, no memories of him haunting her mind the way Pete's last act had haunted her for the longest time. "I gave you a way out."

She paused for a second, trying to pull herself together, to focus on her words and not the horrible, sick feeling they created within her.

"So just take it, will you?" Her mind scrambling from point to point, she thought of what had brought her to him in the first place. He was paying her for a job. "I know I'm not quite finished decorating your house, but Nathan can take over."

For a second, Simon had no idea who she was talking about. And then he remembered. "Nathan being the tall, skinny guy with the large ears?"

She nodded. "He's very good," she told him, then with effort, added, "You won't be disappointed."

He looked at her for a very long moment that seemed to melt into oblivion.

"I wouldn't count on that," he told her, his voice so low it was almost inaudible.

He didn't know what else to say. He'd come here, feeling like a man who was trying to cross over an expanse of quicksand, wanting to either straighten things out or permanently set them aside. Simon felt as if he'd done neither. If anything, he was more confused than ever. But pushing matters right now, especially with a woman who seemed determined to flee from him, didn't seem like the way to go.

She needed time and so did he.

So, without another word to her, Simon turned away and walked out through the door.

The final *click* echoed endlessly over and over in her brain.

Kennon stood there, staring at the door after it had closed. Feeling as if she had just been punched hard in the stomach and was unable to breathe.

This was what she knew would come to pass, what she had tried to precipitate early because then, she'd told herself, it wouldn't hurt nearly so much as it would down the line. Like a preemptive strike.

But there'd been a part of her that wanted—desperately wanted—Simon to negate all her fears, to effectively blast them out of the water by sweeping her into his arms, telling her that she was being ridiculous and that she was the one, the *only* one, who could make him feel glad again that he was alive.

But he hadn't.

Instead, Simon had taken the out she'd given him and just walked away.

Taken it? Hell, he'd fairly grabbed it, pressed it to his chest and all but run out the door. Everything but shouting "Hallelujah!" as he made his getaway.

A getaway she had handed him on a silver platter.

She felt her eyes tear up and she clenched her fingernails into her hands, squeezing them hard, hoping that would somehow squeeze the tears back so that they wouldn't fall.

"I do *not* have big ears."

She swung around to see Nathan all but marching into the showroom.

Upset, frustrated, Kennon redirected everything that she was feeling at her assistant. "I *asked* you to go to the storeroom."

His face was the picture of combined indignation and innocence. "I did."

"Then how did you hear him say that?" she demanded angrily.

In response, he pointed to the wall just behind her. Specifically, to the upper portion close to the ceiling. "Vents," he told her simply. "There are vents here, in your office and in the storeroom. In case you don't know, voices have a tendency to carry unless you're whispering." Obviously perturbed by Simon's cursory description, Nathan looked into the black-lacquer-framed mirror. Angling his head first one way, then the other, he frowned critically, displeased by what he saw. "Maybe I should grow my hair long to cover them."

When he didn't receive the expected disclaimer or verbal jab from Kennon, Nathan shifted his eyes to look at her reflection in the mirror. Turning around, he put his arms around her. "Oh, honey, don't cry. This isn't over yet, you'll see." For a brief moment, Kennon struggled and tried to shrug him away. When she couldn't, she surrendered, allowing Nathan to comfort her. "He'll come to his senses," Nathan promised. "Hopefully, so will you," he added, supposedly under his breath, but deliberately loud enough to make sure that she heard.

Kennon took a breath and this time succeeded in drawing away. She squared her shoulders. She had no time for self-pity. She'd survived Pete, she could certainly survive this. After all, she'd invested so much more time in Pete.

Her heart hurt so much, she could barely stand it.

Still, somehow she managed to say to Nathan, "We've got work to do."

There were still several outstanding details to address at Simon's house before she felt her obligations had been met. She'd meant what she'd said about having Nathan take over. But given her assistant's penchant for allowing his feelings to color his judgment, she knew she would have to supervise Nathan's choices. She just couldn't be there to see how it all came together.

Right now she wasn't strong enough to face that. Or Simon and his daughters.

He was attempting to make sense out of a paper that had just been published outlining a new approach to a surgical procedure that burned away a minimum of damaged heart tissue in order to help control unwanted palpitations. Attempting, but he just couldn't get himself to focus, to concentrate.

He'd been on the same short paragraph for half an hour now.

With a self-deprecating sigh, he glanced up and saw that Meghan stood in the doorway of his office, her small arms crossed before her even smaller chest.

"What's up?" he asked her, for the moment setting the paper back on his desk. Maybe he'd absorb more of it later, he thought.

Meghan frowned. "Why isn't she here, Daddy?" she asked.

It had been eight days since he'd gone to the show-room to see Kennon, gone to see her without really knowing what he would say until it was out of his mouth. Not that anything he'd said had made any sense. He'd come away feeling that maybe he and Kennon really *weren't* meant to be together.

He'd done his best to put her out of his mind and go on with his life. But she refused to stay out of his thoughts, refused to fade into the background. When he least expected it, she would pop up in his thoughts to haunt him. And, those rare times when she didn't, he would catch one of the girls looking at him as if he'd committed some vast transgression.

He'd counted himself lucky that they didn't press him for details, but apparently, looking at Meghan now, his grace period was officially over.

"Doesn't she like us anymore?" Meghan asked when he didn't answer her first question.

Before Kennon had so briefly come into their lives, he would have brushed Meghan off with a comment about how this was a "grown-up" matter not to be discussed with children. But he realized now that that would have been insulting. Meghan and Madelyn were people, same as he, with feelings. Same as he. The last thing he wanted was for his daughters to feel that they were lacking, especially since this was no fault of theirs.

"Oh, no, she likes you," he assured his younger daughter. When she continued looking at him expectantly, he added, "She's just busy."

"Busy doing what?"

"Her job." He saw that his answer didn't come close to satisfying Meghan. "Kennon decorates houses, you know that. And she's finished with ours." *And me,* he added silently.

"Can't we tell her we need something else?" she suggested hopefully.

Yes, like needing to see her face the first thing in the morning, he thought. *Needing to see her the last thing at night.*

He upbraided himself for allowing his thoughts to stray like that. Nothing would be gained by clinging to a baseless hope like that. It just made a person more miserable in the long run.

"But we don't, honey, you know that," Simon pointed out.

"Yes, we do," Madelyn contradicted. She'd been standing in the hallway, out of sight, listening to the exchange between her father and her sister. But now she stepped into the doorway, determined to get her father to do something about this situation.

"And what do we need her for, Madelyn?" he asked gamely, curious despite himself to hear what she had to say.

Madelyn never hesitated. "You need her to make you not sad again." Frowning, Madelyn took a deep breath and then launched into her explanation. "Mommy never liked it when you were sad, Daddy. She always wanted you to be happy. Kennon made you laugh." She glanced at her sister for backup. "She made all of us laugh." Meghan bobbed her head up and down in fierce agreement. "And that's a good thing, right?" Madelyn pressed, asking her father. When he slowly nodded, she pushed on. "Mommy would have liked Kennon, I know she would have," she insisted. "So it's okay for us to like her, too. Please, Daddy, can Kennon come back? She'll come back if you ask her to," she told him, with the certainty of the very young who could still see the world in uncomplicated terms.

He hadn't been that young in a very long time.

Simon shook his head. "I don't think she wants to come back." Both his daughters were staring at him now, and neither looked convinced. "I said some things to make her go away."

"Then un-say them," Meghan pleaded.

Madelyn seemed to see that he didn't believe it was that easy. She added weight to her sister's plea. "Mommy always said that if you say you're sorry, *really* sorry, the bad things you did or said aren't so bad anymore. If you're sorry enough, they go away."

Simon looked at his older daughter for a long moment. *Out of the mouths of babes.* His eight-year-old had just put into words what he'd been feeling. Made him face what he'd tried to ignore. Kennon had made him feel happy for the first time in thirteen months. Made him so happy that it had scared him.

Because he was afraid that happiness would be yanked away from him, just as it had been before, when his wife had died. But rather than protect himself from pain, distancing himself from Kennon had only brought it on in spades. It made him realize that a little bit of happiness was better than his current dark, formless state.

Better for him and better for his girls.

They deserved to have a happy father—and he deserved Kennon. If he'd known what lay ahead, he wouldn't have allowed Nancy to go in his place. And he wouldn't have gone, either. But Nancy *had* elected to go and life had dealt him—and the girls—a very harsh hand.

But now life had shuffled the cards again, promising him a better hand for however long he could hang on to it.

Maybe for the rest of his life.

He looked at Madelyn and then smiled at her. "How did you get so smart?"

Her worried look fading, Madelyn puffed up her chest. "Mommy made me smart."

Rising, he crossed to her and gave the girl a quick hug. Displays of feelings also had come more easily to him after Kennon had entered their lives. They all owed that woman a vote of thanks. And more.

"She certainly did," he agreed.

"Me, too!" Meghan piped up, not wanting to be left out.

He smiled and nodded. "Yes, you, too."

The very fact that he could embrace his daughters, laugh with them, was also Kennon's doing. She'd taught him to be more open with his girls, to listen to them when they spoke. And to treat them like pint-size human beings. He couldn't just let a woman like that, who could open both his eyes *and* his heart, slip right through his fingers because of his inability to leap into action.

It was time for him to leap.

"Edna," he called out to the nanny. Edna had arrived back home three days after he and Kennon had parted company. She'd brought pictures of her brand-new grandnephew and immediately noted the somber atmosphere. "I need to go out for a little while."

Edna seemed to materialize out of thin air, approaching them. "To see Miss Kennon, I hope."

He looked at her, taken a little aback. Was everyone part of this conspiracy to bring Kennon and him together? "You, too?" he asked, not bothering to hide his smile.

"Me, too," she assured him.

"I'd better get on my way, then."

"I was just thinking that," she said, all but physically pushing him out the door.

Chapter Sixteen

It wasn't pressure that finally caused Kennon to rethink her position and surrender.

At least, not outer pressure. This, despite the fact that Nathan had developed the annoying ability to make almost every other comment out of his mouth somehow refer back to Simon. It wasn't even her mother, who called every day—sometimes twice a day—to "chat" and ask how "things" were going. The "chats" always ended with her mother asking Kennon how much longer she would waste time before coming to her senses.

Though both things very nearly drove her up the wall, neither was responsible for her caving. What finally did it was that she missed Simon. Missed him desperately. Missed him *and* his daughters far more than she thought humanly possible. The raw ache inside her grew until it all but swallowed her whole and made it impossible for her to concentrate. She was no good to herself or to anyone else in this state and she had to act.

She missed Simon infinitely more than she'd *ever* missed Pete, even initially. She couldn't allow herself to endure this self-imposed life sentence of what amounted to solitary confinement. She would break out of jail and make a run for it, back to Simon and the girls. Hopefully, once she'd done that, she'd find a way to work things out, make Simon want her. She was confident the girls were in her corner.

Or would be once she apologized to them for disappearing this way.

Right in the middle of searching for the perfect accent pieces to go with her present client's newly added game room, Kennon left the cavernous discount house, got into her car and headed straight to Simon's house like an arrow to its target.

It had been eight days since they'd seen each other and it felt like an eternity.

The Bedford police department appeared to be otherwise occupied and nowhere in sight, which was fortunate because Kennon had raced all the way there, squeaking through yellow lights by less than a breath at times.

A cauldron of emotions spilled over her the instant she saw his house.

Anticipation swirled through her. *Please don't make this hard,* she prayed, parking.

Kennon didn't see Simon's car in the driveway, but that was all right. The garage door was closed. She knew from experience that Simon preferred parking his vehicle inside the garage to keep the car clean longer.

For a man, he was incredibly neat—in every possible definition of the word.

Nerves danced wickedly through her as she rang the doorbell. Her fingertips felt clammy as she found herself praying that it wasn't too late.

Praying that Simon hadn't decided that she'd been right to create this separation between them.

Edna's smile was spontaneous and warm, not to mention wide, when she opened the door and saw her standing there. Kennon's nervousness evaporated immediately.

"Miss Kennon, how *are* you?" the nanny asked, then urged, "Come in, come in," before Kennon had a chance to answer her.

The moment she stepped over the threshold, Kennon found herself encircled by two pairs of small arms and on the receiving end of fierce hugs and raised, happy voices. Madelyn and Meghan, drawn by Edna's greeting, had both flown to the door to see for themselves if their beloved Kennon had returned.

"You came, you came," Meghan cried happily, hugging her so hard the little girl became utterly breathless.

"Dad *did* it!" Madelyn declared in triumph. "He did go and get you!"

Touched by the profusion of love, Kennon drew back slightly, although she kept one arm tucked around each little girl. She tried to make sense out of what Madelyn was saying.

"Your dad's not here?" Even as she asked, Kennon scanned the room. Disappointment burrowed through her.

In response, Madelyn peered around her torso and

tilted her head as she looked outside the door. She answered Kennon's question with another question. "He's not coming with you?"

"No. Why?" Kennon did her best not to sound as nervous as she felt. "Did your father say he was going to?"

She looked up at Edna for an explanation.

"Dr. Simon told the girls that he was going to go see you." Edna paused for a moment, then lowered her voice as she moved in closer, trying to share her thought with only Kennon. "My guess is that he was coming to apologize for doing whatever it was that he did to make you leave."

"He didn't do anything," Kennon said, feeling guilty that he'd even thought he had. "It was my fault," she admitted, then delicately extricated herself from her two biggest fans. "I'd better try to catch him."

Rather than agree or wish her luck, the tall, sturdy woman placed a large hand on Kennon's shoulder and held her in place.

"My suggestion is to stay right here. Dr. Simon does have to return home at some point, and if you leave and try to catch up with him, I can see the man doing the same the minute the little ones tell him you were here." She eyed Kennon sympathetically. "The two of you could spend an entire lifetime missing one another, just like in that old, frustrating poem, *Evangeline*. Why don't you just stay here with us until Dr. Simon comes back?" she suggested, with the confidence of a woman who knew she was right.

It made sense, Kennon thought as she nodded. "All right, I'll stay here and wait."

The second that was settled, Meghan piped up, "Did you miss us?"

With children, there was no need for games, or secrets. Children responded well to the truth. "Terribly," Kennon assured both girls. Once again she put an arm around each set of small shoulders. "More than you can possibly ever know."

"We missed you, too," Madelyn reported solemnly. For good measure, she crossed her heart.

Hopefully, Simon had missed her, too, Kennon thought. She did her best to focus only on the girls and not let her mind drift over to thoughts of Simon and questions that began: "What if—?" She'd find out "what if" soon enough.

Simon swallowed the curse that hovered on his lips.

Kennon's shop was closed down for the night when he got there. Looking in through the showroom window had yielded no telltale back-office light, no light at all to indicate that she might be somewhere on the premises.

He was confronted with the same dead end when he arrived at her house. There wasn't even a front porch light on to indicate that she was coming back this evening.

Could she have taken off on a trip somewhere? Just like that? he asked himself uneasily.

Was there someone else?

Simon tried her cell. It went to voice mail after four rings. Three frustrating times.

Calling her landline yielded another runaround episode. This time he got to listen to her voice on the answering machine. "If you'd like to leave a message—"

"No, I wouldn't like to leave a damn message," he growled under his breath. "I want to talk to you in person. I want to hold you and make love with you until you realize we belong together."

Suddenly aware that the answering machine was picking all this up, he slapped his cell phone shut, terminating the call.

Great. Now she would think he was crazy and take out a restraining order against him.

Frustrated, Simon paced in her driveway and debated waiting in front of her house until she finally came back, but if she *was* off on a trip somewhere, heaven only knew how long she'd be gone. He couldn't just wait out here like some mooning, lovesick teenager. He had a life to lead. A life that didn't feel as if it was a proper fit anymore, not without her in it.

Simon sighed, dragging his hand through his hair. He had to be getting back to the girls. Somehow, he was going to have to find a way to explain to them why he wasn't returning home with the woman all three of them had fallen in love with.

There, he thought, starting up the car again, he'd said it. Admitted it without having his arm twisted, albeit silently and to himself, but it was a start. He loved Kennon. And he wanted to have a chance at spending forever with her.

But first, he told himself, he had to find her.

After he got home and talked to the girls. He didn't want them waiting and worrying.

Lost in thought, Simon didn't register the car at the curb as he glanced toward it without seeing it. He pulled into the garage and depressed the garage door remote.

The door was on its way down when he realized what he'd seen. Springing to life, he darted outside. The garage door came within a hair's breadth of closing on him before it stopped moving, shuddered and then went back up again.

That was Kennon's car. He recognized the make, as well as the license number.

Was she here? Had she come looking for him while he'd been out trying to find her so that they could talk?

Or was there some other reason Kennon was here?

He didn't care about the reason. Whatever had brought her back was fine with him. All he wanted was to make use of the opportunity and talk her into reconsidering walking out of his life.

Most of all, he wanted to talk Kennon into giving him another chance. He wanted to be able to make the right sort of impression this time around, to change her life the way she'd changed his—and the lives of his girls.

The moment he opened the door leading from the garage into the house, his daughters came running over to him, excitement pulsating through them as well as the atmosphere they generated around them.

"She's here, she's here!" Their young voices melded together as they excitedly shouted out the announcement to him.

Each girl grabbed one of his hands and pulled mightily, leading him into the living room.

Simon didn't remember walking. One second the girls were coming at him, the next he was in the living room, facing Kennon, wanting nothing more than to sweep her into his arms.

Well, maybe *one* thing more. But if he kissed her now, he might not be able to stop, so he refrained.

Kennon watched him a little uneasily, not quite certain how to gauge his reaction to her being here. "I didn't mean to barge in—"

He spoke over her. "I went to your store. Then your house—"

Two voices undercut one another, dueling for space and to be heard exclusively. "I'm sorry, I didn't mean what I said—"

He shook his head, negating the part he heard her say. "I should have come to you sooner—"

They continued talking over one another, mixing words, sentences, emotions. The two little girls looked at one another, clearly frustrated.

Madelyn stepped in between them, pressing a small hand against each of them. "Stop talking and kiss each other," she pleaded.

Mutually struck by the absurdity of the situation—and how confusing it had to seem to the girls—Simon and Kennon stopped talking and laughed.

Kennon glanced at the man who had won her heart without even trying. "You have a very smart daughter."

She'd get no argument from him. "I'm just beginning to find that out."

Tired of being on the sidelines, Meghan got behind Kennon and pushed her toward Simon.

Not to be outdone, Madelyn got behind her father and pushed him toward Kennon.

Neither had to work too hard to achieve their goal.

"Ask her, Daddy. Ask her!" begged Meghan, a budding matchmaker.

"Yeah," Madelyn chimed in. "Ask her before she changes her mind again."

He hadn't intended for his confrontation with Kennon to be a group effort. And he certainly hadn't intended for the two pint-size women in his life to steal the thunder of what had been hovering in the back of his mind for the last week, especially as he began mourning the demise of a relationship that had never been allowed to flourish and take serious root.

Impatient that her father wasn't being fast enough, Meghan took the lead and put the all-important question to Kennon. "Will you be our mommy?"

Stunned, Kennon felt a wave of heat pass over her even as a sense of longing, mixed with joy, surged through her.

But the question wasn't coming from Simon, it was coming from his daughter, she reminded herself. All the man probably wanted was just some sort of a temporary relationship. But at least it was a *relationship*. And that was a start.

Simon looked down at his younger child and did his best to sound stern. Before Kennon had come into their lives, it wouldn't have taken any effort at all to sound that way because he *was* stern. She'd mellowed him. And he was grateful.

"Meghan, you can't put Kennon on the spot like that," Simon told her.

Madelyn came to her sister's defense. "But you're not asking her, Daddy," the older girl complained. "So we have to help." She took her place beside Meghan and turned large, luminous and, above all, pleading eyes on Kennon. "Will you?"

With all her heart, she wanted to shout yes, but she

was afraid that if she showed too much enthusiasm, it would make Simon back off again. So she chose her words carefully.

"I can tell you that I'll always be there for you when you need me," Kennon hedged.

Meghan shook her head. "But you *gotta* marry Daddy. That's part of the deal," she stressed.

Chagrined, Simon didn't know where to begin. He looked at Kennon and apologized.

"I'm sorry about putting you on the spot like this." He looked at his daughters, but for the life of him, he couldn't be stern right now, especially since he understood how they felt.

Because he felt the same way.

"Don't be," she told him, then looked away in case he saw too much in her eyes. "It's nice being wanted that much."

He'd never get a better opening than that, he thought. "Well, in that case…"

She could have sworn her heart hitched in her chest just then. "Yes?"

He'd always been the type who'd known what he wanted when he finally saw it. Granted he'd been a little slower this time around, but that was because he was still coming to terms with the upheaval in his life. But now that was settled and he was focused again. He knew that Kennon was the woman he wanted to be with. Knew it the way he'd known when he'd first been with Nancy.

And what made it feel even more right was that he felt certain Nancy would have approved. She'd always wanted him and the girls to be happy. And Kennon made them happy. More than that, Kennon had succeeded in making them a real family again.

"If I asked," he said slowly, "what would your answer be?"

Oh no, she wasn't going to expose herself like that, not without Simon saying *something* more binding than that. "Depends on *what* you asked," she told him.

All right, she'd taught him about what it took to be a family, about the importance of being together, and all that was well and good. But there were some moments that needed privacy, without a cheering section.

He turned to his older daughter. "Madelyn, take your sister into the family room and play with her, please."

Madelyn gave every impression of being right there for the long haul. "We don't want to play anything, Daddy, we—"

Edna swept into the room seemingly out of nowhere. "You heard your father, girls, you need to leave Miss Kennon and him alone for a bit." As she spoke, she began to usher the two sisters out of the room quickly.

Meghan gave in to the inevitable, but she looked over her shoulder at Kennon as she was being led out of the room. "Will you still be here later?"

Kennon stole a covert look at Simon, then shifted her eyes back to Meghan. "I think there's a very good chance I might be," she told Meghan. As they were taken from the room, Kennon dropped her voice and asked Simon, "Does Edna always materialize that way, just at the right moment?"

He nodded. "Pretty much. It's written into her contract."

The corners of Kennon's mouth curved. "You've developed a sense of humor."

"That was your doing," he admitted. "As was my learning to spend more than a few minutes at a time with the girls." Simon paused. "I'm getting sidetracked again."

"And what's the main track?"

"They want you to be their mother."

And? her mind whispered. "I know," she said out loud. "I was listening."

And he should be talking, Simon thought. He took a breath, then let it out slowly. "I've only done this once before and I'm not very good at it."

Mentally, she crossed her fingers—and prayed.

"Give it a shot," she said encouragingly. Though she knew she shouldn't let herself get carried away, at this point she couldn't keep from hoping that this was going where she so desperately wanted it to go.

Here goes nothing, Simon thought. "You not only made me find a sense of humor and taught me how important it is to be part of a family unit, how important it is to be a father to my daughters, you also brought me back from the dead."

She felt herself growing nervous again. "And all before breakfast, too," she quipped.

He found that he could read her. The thought was comforting. "Now, that's nervous humor."

Kennon nodded. "That it is." She waited. The pause grew longer. "Are you trying to ask me something?"

"No," he answered seriously. "I'm trying to tell you something." He watched her expression as he continued. "I'm trying to tell you that I love you. That your coming into our lives made everything I just said possible. I know that I have no right to put you on the spot any more than Meghan did—"

"I'll be the judge of that," she said, interrupting him. "Some of us work best when we're put on the spot. Go ahead," she urged.

"Okay." Why was his mouth so dry all of a sudden? "Will you marry me?"

"Could you go back to the 'love' part?" she requested with a warm smile. "I like hearing that part."

The request made him realize something. "I haven't heard you say anything about love."

"Then you haven't been paying attention." Because she realized she'd been conveying just that message with every fiber of her being for a while now. She'd told him without the benefit of actual words.

Kennon wove her arms around his neck. "But for the record, yes, I love you. Yes, I love the girls—and I even love Edna, too," she threw in for good measure. "And, yes, I will be their mommy and, yes, I will marry you," she concluded, letting out a long breath. "Does that cover everything?" she asked with a wicked smile.

Simon drew her closer and could feel the heat of her body against his. "Does for me."

He had only begun to kiss Kennon when his daughters came running back into the room, squealing and cheering loudly.

"I thought Edna took you to the family room to play," he said, looking at them over his shoulder. "Were you standing outside the room and listening?" he asked. He did his best to look at them as sternly as he once had.

"No, Daddy," they protested in unison.

"It has something to do with vents," Kennon told him just before she turned his head back toward her. "C'mere, you. I'm not finished with you yet."

And she wouldn't be, he thought as he sealed his lips to hers. Not for at least a lifetime.

Maybe more.

And in the background, he thought he heard Meghan ask, "*Now* can we go to Knott's Berry Farm?" He could feel his heart smiling.

* * * * *

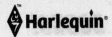**Harlequin**®

COMING NEXT MONTH

Available May 31, 2011

SPECIAL EDITION

#2119 FORTUNE FOUND
Victoria Pade
The Fortunes of Texas: Lost...and Found

#2120 HUSBAND UNDER CONSTRUCTION
Karen Templeton
Wed in the West

#2121 DADDY'S DOUBLE DUTY
Stella Bagwell
Men of the West

#2122 WHAT THE SINGLE DAD WANTS...
Marie Ferrarella
Matchmaking Mamas

#2123 A HOME FOR THE M.D.
Gina Wilkins
Doctors in the Family

#2124 THE TEXAS TYCOON'S BABY
Crystal Green
Billionaire Cowboys, Inc.

HSECNM0511

REQUEST YOUR FREE BOOKS!
2 FREE NOVELS PLUS 2 FREE GIFTS!

◆ **Harlequin**®

SPECIAL EDITION
Life, Love & Family

YES! Please send me 2 FREE Harlequin Special Edition® novels and my 2 FREE gifts (gifts are worth about $10). After receiving them, if I don't wish to receive any more books, I can return the shipping statement marked "cancel." If I don't cancel, I will receive 6 brand-new novels every month and be billed just $4.24 per book in the U.S. or $4.99 per book in Canada. That's a saving of at least 15% off the cover price! It's quite a bargain! Shipping and handling is just 50¢ per book in the U.S. and 75¢ per book in Canada.* I understand that accepting the 2 free books and gifts places me under no obligation to buy anything. I can always return a shipment and cancel at any time. Even if I never buy another book, the two free books and gifts are mine to keep forever.

235/335 SDN FC7H

Name _____ (PLEASE PRINT) _____

Address _____ Apt. # _____

City _____ State/Prov. _____ Zip/Postal Code _____

Signature (if under 18, a parent or guardian must sign)

Mail to the **Reader Service**:
IN U.S.A.: P.O. Box 1867, Buffalo, NY 14240-1867
IN CANADA: P.O. Box 609, Fort Erie, Ontario L2A 5X3

Not valid for current subscribers to Harlequin Special Edition books.

Want to try two free books from another line?
Call 1-800-873-8635 or visit www.ReaderService.com.

* Terms and prices subject to change without notice. Prices do not include applicable taxes. Sales tax applicable in N.Y. Canadian residents will be charged applicable taxes. Offer not valid in Quebec. This offer is limited to one order per household. All orders subject to credit approval. Credit or debit balances in a customer's account(s) may be offset by any other outstanding balance owed by or to the customer. Please allow 4 to 6 weeks for delivery. Offer available while quantities last.

Your Privacy—The Reader Service is committed to protecting your privacy. Our Privacy Policy is available online at www.ReaderService.com or upon request from the Reader Service.

We make a portion of our mailing list available to reputable third parties that offer products we believe may interest you. If you prefer that we not exchange your name with third parties, or if you wish to clarify or modify your communication preferences, please visit us at www.ReaderService.com/consumerschoice or write to us at Reader Service Preference Service, P.O. Box 9062, Buffalo, NY 14269. Include your complete name and address.

HSE11

Harlequin® Blaze™ brings you
New York Times *and* USA TODAY *bestselling author*
Vicki Lewis Thompson with three new steamy titles
from the bestselling miniseries SONS OF CHANCE

Chance isn't just the last name of these rugged
Wyoming cowboys—it's their motto, too!

Read on for a sneak peek at the first title,
SHOULD'VE BEEN A COWBOY

Available June 2011 only from Harlequin® Blaze™.

"THANKS FOR NOT TURNING ON THE LIGHTS," Tyler said. "I'm a mess."

"Not in my book." Even in low light, Alex had a good view of her yellow shirt plastered to her body. It was all he could do not to reach for her, mud and all. But the next move needed to be hers, not his.

She slicked her wet hair back and squeezed some water out of the ends as she glanced upward. "I like the sound of the rain on a tin roof."

"Me, too."

She met his gaze briefly and looked away. "Where's the sink?"

"At the far end, beyond the last stall."

Tyler's running shoes squished as she walked down the aisle between the rows of stalls. She glanced sideways at Alex. "So how much of a cowboy are you these days? Do you ride the range and stuff?"

"I ride." He liked being able to say that. "Why?"

"Just wondered. Last summer, you were still a city boy. You even told me you weren't the cowboy type, but you're…different now."

He wasn't sure if that was a good thing or a bad thing. Maybe she preferred city boys to cowboys. "How am I different?"

"Well, you dress differently, and your hair's a little longer. Your face seems a little more chiseled, but maybe that's because of your hair. Also, there's something else, something harder to define, an attitude…"

"Are you saying I have an attitude?"

"Not in a bad way. It's more like a quiet confidence."

He was flattered, but still he had to laugh. "I just admitted a while ago that I have all kinds of doubts about this event tomorrow. That doesn't seem like quiet confidence to me."

"This isn't about your job, it's about…your…" She took a deep breath. "It's about your sex appeal, okay? I have no business talking about it, because it will only make me want to do things I shouldn't do." She started toward the end of the barn. "Now, where's that sink? We need to get cleaned up and go back to the house. Dinner is probably ready, and I—"

He spun her around and pulled her into his arms, mud and all. "Let's do those things." Then he kissed her, knowing that she would kiss him back, knowing that this time he would take that kiss where he wanted it to go. And she would let him.

Follow Tyler and Alex's wild adventures in
SHOULD'VE BEEN A COWBOY
Available June 2011 only from Harlequin® Blaze™
wherever books are sold.

HBEXP0611